She'd wanted. *Him.*

The thought sent blood rushing to her cheeks and formed a knot in her stomach.

"What are you thinking to make you blush like that?"

His voice, throaty and amused, drew her attention back to the face she'd been staring at. "N-nothing."

Then came the smug, cocky grin that used to make her want to smack him. "Were you imagining me naked?" He raised his hands in a helpless shrug, when he was anything but. "Women usually do. Better yet, were you imagining *us* naked? Because I have been, and that sofa makes into a damn comfortable bed."

Slowly she shook her head. "I don't think so." It was eye-opening just how tempted she was, even though there were a thousand reasons why she shouldn't be. It was risky. What if the Justin she loved to hate came back? What if this thing *was* just the side effect of adrenaline and fear? What kind of potential was there between her and Justin? Besides great sex.

And the biggest question: Was she willing to risk having her heart broken again?

Dear Reader,

Writers find inspiration everywhere, so it was no surprise that I came back from my first visit to Cozumel with Justin and Cate's story forming in my head. It's no surprise, either, with avid divers filling my world, that Justin is one, too. I didn't get to even dip a toe into the water on that first trip, but I made up for it on the next, going snorkeling several times with my husband and my best friend. It was a great experience that gave me a taste of Justin's passion for the ocean.

Of course, his passion for diving doesn't begin to match his passion for Cate. In the beginning that emotion is expressed more along the lines of dislike, a feeling that she wholeheartedly shares, and with good reason. What fun it was turning them around from "not in this lifetime" to "happily ever after!"

Marilyn

MARILYN PAPPANO

In the Enemy's Arms

ROMANTIC
SUSPENSE

Recycling programs
for this product may
not exist in your area.

ISBN-13: 978-0-373-27782-7

IN THE ENEMY'S ARMS

Books by Marilyn Pappano

Harlequin Romantic Suspense

MARILYN PAPPANO

has spent most of her life growing into the person she was meant to be, but isn't there yet. She's been blessed by family—her husband, their son, his lovely wife and a grandson who is almost certainly the most beautiful and talented baby in the world—and friends, along with a writing career that's made her one of the luckiest people around. Her passions, besides those already listed, include the pack of wild dogs who make their home in her house, fighting the good fight against the weeds that make up her yard, killing the creepy-crawlies that slither out of those weeds and, of course, anything having to do with books.

For my favorite divers: my son Brandon;
Meg Reid, dive master and best friend; and, as always,
to my husband, Bob. One of these days I'm going to
join you guys under the sea!

And until that day,
major thanks to my non-dive buddy, Don Shidler,
for keeping me company onshore!

Chapter 1

Welcome to Cozumel, the flight attendant had said as the jet taxied to a stop. The uniformed men armed with deadly weapons between the plane and the terminal weren't Cate Calloway's idea of a perfect welcoming party, but their presence didn't unnerve her as it had on her first trip to the Mexican island.

Taking a deep breath of warm humid air and smiling at the soldiers who never smiled back, she towed her bag behind her and went inside. She'd sent her supplies ahead, so she made it through immigration, baggage and customs fairly quickly. In the small lobby at the front of the building, she stood away from the flow of eager tourists to scan the area.

There was no sign of Trent or Susanna and not even a vaguely familiar face in the room. A number of men waited, holding signs with the names of the parties they were picking up, but none of them was looking for her.

After ten minutes, she made herself comfortable against the wall. After twenty minutes, she pulled out her cell phone, grateful that she'd bothered with the international calling plan for this trip, and dialed Trent's number. It went straight to voice mail. So did Susanna's.

After thirty minutes, she found a taxi driver, showed him the address of La Casa and climbed into the backseat. She didn't mind being forgotten at the airport in a country where she barely spoke the language and having to make her own way to La Casa. Really, she wasn't that petty. It was just that on her previous trips, Trent had met her himself. She'd never gone anywhere alone. It had been easier to feel independent with him or Susanna there beside her.

The cabdriver wasn't chatty, but that was okay. The Louisiana divers who'd surrounded her on the airplane had been chatty enough to give her a new appreciation for silence. He swerved through crowded streets, narrowly missing cars and scooters alike, until traffic thinned as they reached the more isolated neighborhood of La Casa.

A tall cinder-block wall surrounded the few acres, with a rusted iron gate standing open next to the drive. The sign identifying the place was so discreet as to go unnoticed: La Casa para Nuestras Hijas. The House for Our Daughters.

Her fourth time here, and Cate was still bemused by the thought of Trent Calloway, her lazy, spoiled, self-centered ex-husband, committing his time, money and self to a shelter for runaway, orphaned or mistreated girls. Granted, he did it out of love—for Susanna, or so he said—but still…

The driver pulled to a stop in front of the house, jumped out and retrieved her bag from the trunk. She traded cash for it, thanking him, then turned to look around. Several buildings hunkered within the walls. The house stood to the left of the drive, once grand with two stories, elaborate ironwork, red-tile roof and deeply shaded porch. In the middle at the rear was a garage that housed school desks, chalkboards and supplies instead of vehicles, and to the right of the drive, also set farther back than the house, was the dormitory, a low squat building whose only ornamentation came from the bright paint on its cinder-block walls: turquoise, sunny yellow, apple red, lime green.

The quiet raised goose bumps on Cate's arms. Usually there was laughter, music, voices. If the girls weren't in class, they were studying under the trees or playing in the grass. There was always a volunteer or two with them, helping with their lessons or organizing games, keeping their spirits up or making them laugh.

"Hello?" she called out. *"¿Hola?"*

Nothing.

Dragging her bag with her, she climbed the two steps to the porch, where the boxes she'd shipped earlier were stacked against the wall. They were filled with medical supplies, from basics like bandages and antiseptics to IV solution and antibiotics. What she didn't use in her two weeks here would be stored or shared with La Casa's other shelters on the mainland.

The front door stood open. She pulled on the screen door, her suitcase bumping over the threshold, then let it close behind her with a thump. "Trent? Susanna? Are you here?"

A sound came from upstairs, like the echo of her suitcase wheels on hardwood floor. A moment later, a woman appeared, staring over the railing as she dragged her own bag along.

Relief rushed through Cate. "GayAnne. I'm glad to see you. Where is everybody?"

GayAnne's bag thudded its way behind her down the stairs. "Gone. Everyone's gone."

"Gone where?"

"Jill and Kyla went home last week to visit their families, and I woke up this morning to find Marta packing up the kids to take to some relative's house. I don't know what's going on, but I'm leaving, too. I'm staying with my boyfriend until everyone comes back."

Marta was a local woman, Cate knew from past visits, the one in charge when Susanna and Trent were busy. She was as dedicated to the girls as Susanna; they were safe with her. "Where is Trent?"

GayAnne shook her head. "Gone. Disappeared. Him and Susanna both." She was about as far from the stereotypical California girl as she could be: petite, red-haired, skin as pale as if it had never seen the sun. The bag she dragged was more than big enough to carry *her,* and the look in her wide blue eyes suggested she might be more comfortable hiding inside. "If I knew anything, I'd tell you, but I don't. If you see Susanna—" the redhead swallowed visibly "—tell her I'm sorry to run out like this, but I'm not staying here alone." She finished with a shrug, avoiding Cate's hand as she passed.

"Wait, GayAnne—"

A horn beeped outside, punctuated by the slamming of the screen door behind GayAnne. "Can't," she called over her shoulder. "No time."

Leaving her own bag where it was, Cate walked to the door. A young man was swinging off a scooter out front. He tossed a second helmet to GayAnne, then heaved her bag onto the back of the scooter, securing it while she strapped on the helmet. A moment later, they were roaring out the gate, and the silence returned.

Cate swallowed hard, and her stomach knotted. Where was Trent? Susanna? The other volunteers? Where were the girls La Casa was built to serve? What in hell was going on here?

Slowly she turned away from the door again. Compared to La Casa's usual activity, everything seemed unnaturally still. The house not only appeared abandoned, it *felt* it. It felt…lost. The sheen of the ancient wood floors seemed duller than usual. The paint on the thick plastered walls looked more faded. The very air smelled empty. Unused.

It unsettled her deep inside.

Her stomach still tight, she walked to the door of the room that served as La Casa's office, making as little noise as possible—as if there were anyone around to hear it. Trent might have just taken off, even though he had obligations here, even though he'd known for six months she would be arriving today. He'd always been lazy and spoiled and selfish. He'd run out on her when things got tough more times than she could count, including that last time. The time she'd filed for divorce.

But Susanna Hunter, God love her, didn't have a lazy, spoiled or selfish bone in her body. She'd been volunteering at soup kitchens when she was a kid, tutoring at-risk children when she was still in school, mentoring, fundraising, *serving*. This place and the girls it cared for meant the world to her. She would never just leave them.

Maybe GayAnne was wrong. Maybe she had a flair for the dramatic that Cate had missed seeing on her last visit. Maybe…

Susanna had run the shelter from this office, while the rest of the place housed the staff. Usually that included Trent and three or four volunteers from the States. GayAnne had been there the longest, since Cate's first visit. The others came from the college Susanna had attended or one of the churches back home that helped fund the mission, and they stayed anywhere from a week to six months. In addition, a couple of local women worked there, too.

Like the rest of the house, the office had an abandoned look: a half-eaten cookie on a saucer, a cup of coffee long gone cold. As if Susanna had merely taken a break and would be back any moment now. Her desk was covered with papers, but Cate had never seen it otherwise. The bulletin board hanging above it didn't have a scrap of empty space available, and the chairs were piled with stacks of things to be filed—again, normal. Susanna was a hands-on person; she tolerated paperwork because it was an evil necessity.

A second, smaller desk on the other side was almost compulsively neat—not because Trent was, by nature, a neat person but because he opted for the easiest way out and, in this case, that was filing as he went along. The corkboard next to his desk held a calendar, with her arrival and departure dates circled in red, and a half-dozen photographs thumbtacked on randomly. They hadn't changed since her last visit: three of Susanna, two of his parents and brothers and one of himself with Justin Seavers, his best friend from college. Two damn goodlooking men, and together they weren't worth a damn.

She eased the picture from under its tack, as was her habit, and studied it. The first time, Trent had cocked one brow and she'd shrugged. *Just wondering where he hides his horns and pitchfork.* The second time, alone in the office, she'd wondered if anyone had ever taken as quick a dislike to her as Justin had. She wasn't accustomed to scorn at first sight. Usually, she had to do something significant to piss someone off that badly.

The photo had been taken within the last few years, on a boat somewhere off the coast of Cozumel. Both Trent and Justin wore dive skins pulled down to their waists. Though they were roughly the same size, they looked as different as night and day. Trent was dark— hair, eyes, skin; a gift from his Italian mother—and Justin was light—blond hair, café au lait skin and coffee-dark eyes. Though one came from Georgia, the other from Alabama, their lives had been pretty much the same from birth: privileged. The Seaverses had even more money than the Calloways; Justin's sense of entitlement had been even greater than Trent's.

Justin's dislike for Cate had been even stronger than that.

Her cheeks heated, and the knot in her gut eased enough to summon her usual derision for Justin. He'd hated that she wasn't just another of Trent's passing diversions. He hadn't wanted to lose his partying buddy— which he hadn't—and he'd thought she didn't deserve Trent. He'd told her so at the rehearsal dinner the night before the wedding.

Cate hadn't seen him since the following day, and she hoped she never would again.

Still clutching the photo, she turned and looked around the office once more. Maybe she should call the police, or Trent's parents. Maybe she should get out of the house and get the authorities in there before any evidence that might exist was destroyed.

Tell the police what? her little voice scoffed. That her irresponsible ex-husband had forgotten she was supposed to arrive today? That his very responsible girlfriend had actually left the house rather than wait for

Cate to make her way there? As for evidence, didn't that imply a crime? Was there anything in this room to suggest something had happened?

Her eyes couldn't see it, but her gut felt…*something*.

Gradually she became aware of a textural difference beneath her fingertips. Turning the photo over, she found a small Post-it note affixed to the picture, the precise writing in Trent's hand.

C: If anything happens, call him. He'll know what to do.

Call Justin Seavers? Yeah, right. The only times she'd ever called him, she'd been looking for her fiancé/husband when he hadn't returned from a night out with the boys. He'd always been at Justin's place, too hung over to talk to her, Justin had said in that superior tone. He'd told her to go on about her business, that Trent would come home when he was ready. Smug bastard.

And Trent wanted her to turn to him now? What could one lazy, irresponsible trust-fund baby do to help another?

Then she read the note again. *If anything happens…* Finding the shelter empty and silent certainly qualified as *anything*.

He'll know what to do. Maybe Trent had confided in him. Maybe Justin could at least tell her something to report to the police. Maybe he knew where Trent and Susanna were and why everyone else had left.

Gritting her teeth, she stuck the photo back on the bulletin board, opened the lower-left drawer on Trent's desk and pulled out a leather-bound address book. Trent relied on his smartphone for a lot, but he also liked paper-and-ink records. She found the entry she needed, then punched the numbers into her cell with tiny, vicious pokes.

The phone rang once in her ear, followed by a sound from outside the office. Moving the cell away, she took a hesitant step toward the door and listened hard. Music came faintly from somewhere inside the house, and it was moving closer.

Her palms went damp, and her heart stuttered to a stop before breaking into a gallop.

Oh, God, someone else was inside the house!

The ringtone was an Eric Clapton song, about a man on the run, trying to avoid getting swept away by a river of tears. Of course, a woman was his downfall; so often they were, though Justin Seavers had had better luck at avoiding that fate than most guys he knew.

There was no special meaning to the ringtone, though. He'd known Cate would call; the song had been on his phone; it was a thoughtless choice. It didn't mean he'd ever cared—would ever care—enough to run from Cate, and it sure as hell didn't mean she could save him. He wasn't of the opinion that he actually needed saving, at least not anymore.

He silenced the phone as he reached the hall, then stepped through the office doorway. She was standing there, posture rigid, fingers clenched tightly around her cell phone. She was ten inches shorter than him, enough to make him feel like the big, strong protector or, more likely, the overlarge clumsy oaf.

When she recognized him, relief flashed across her face, quickly replaced with the cool, disdainful look she usually reserved just for him. "You," she breathed, letting the tension, or most of it, ease from her body.

Justin leaned against the doorjamb, one ankle crossing the other. "What's up, doc?"

Straightening her spine, she managed to appear an inch or so taller. "Where's Trent? Susanna? Why did all the volunteers leave? What's going on here?"

He shrugged one shoulder. "Don't know."

"What do you mean, you don't know? Trent said—"

"When did you talk to him?"

She blinked, unaccustomed to being interrupted. She might be delicate in size and stature and, according to Trent, sweeter than sugar most of the time, but she was probably the most book-smart person Justin had ever known, and she was accustomed to being in charge. People didn't interrupt Dr. Cate Calloway, head of emergency medicine at the Copper Lake Hospital and part-time instructor of trauma management at her alma mater.

"A week ago. Maybe ten days. I called to let him know I'd shipped some supplies and to see if they needed anything else."

"How did he seem?"

She blinked again. "Like Trent. He was on another call. He said if Susanna thought of something, she'd give me a call. If not, they'd see me today."

"And neither of them called you?"

The effort to stop from rolling her eyes was visible in the tension in her jaw. "No. Otherwise, I would have said *that* was the last time I talked to him—" She drew a breath. "What are you doing here?"

He shrugged again. Annoying her had always come easily to him. All he had to do was breathe. Hippocratic oath or not, he was pretty sure if someone hauled him into her E.R. on the verge of death, she'd be tempted to shove him over.

"I thought I'd see how the diving is this fall."

"Then why aren't you on a boat out in the ocean?"

"My dive buddy's taken some time off. What's in the boxes out there?"

"Medical supplies, toiletries, books, clothes."

"Any drugs?"

The disdain increased fractionally. "Antibiotics, antihistamines, some nonnarcotic pain relievers. Nothing special. Why are you really here? Trent said if anything happened—" She raised her hand when he started to interrupt again. "He wrote in a note that if anything happened, I should call you, and now here you are. How convenient. Why you? Why not the police, his parents, the foundation?"

Ignoring her questions, he finally moved away from the door and into the room. It seemed to shrink by half, putting him closer to her than he'd been in a very long time. "What note?"

The corners of her mouth pinching, she took the few steps to the bulletin board and pulled off the photo from a dive trip three years ago. He barely glanced at it but turned it over to read the note on the back. Looking up again, he cocked his brow. "You two arranged a secret message system involving this photo of me?"

Her mouth pinched even more, as if she'd sucked the sourest of limes. "Of course not. He just knew...I usually...pick up the picture at least once...when I'm here." Her face tinged with a blush, and she was *not* an attractive blusher.

Everything else about her, though...straight brown hair, blunt cut, in a braid today, blue eyes, a mouth to match the sweet nature he'd been told she possessed, great legs, nice body. He'd think she had chosen beach-casual for travel, in brown shorts that showed no curves, a tan tank top that clung to every curve and flat sandals with straps, but she always dressed for comfort. Trent joked that was why she'd gone into medicine in the first place. What could be cozier than wearing scrubs all the time?

He fingered the picture before peeling off the Post-it and crumpling it. "So my picture interests you."

She snorted. "*Puzzles* would be a better word. I look at it and wonder how two men with all the advantages money can buy can grow up to become…well, you and Trent."

He was about to make some flippant reply when a sound outside caught his attention: the crunch of tires on gravel, the low rumble of an engine. Pocketing the picture, he stepped past her to the window, keeping to the side of the flimsy curtains, and lifted one edge just enough to see the black vehicle in the driveway. The first man out was tall, muscle-bound, and he gripped a stubby black pistol. There was no doubt in Justin's mind that he worked for the Wallaces.

Muttering a curse, he grabbed her arm on his way out of the room. "We've got company, and it's sure as hell not a welcoming committee. Come on."

He expected resistance, but she dragged her feet only long enough to grab hold of her suitcase in the middle of the hallway. Yanking it up, she awkwardly shoved the handle in one-handed, then let him pull her down the hall to the back of the house. As they turned into the kitchen to reach the rear door, and the backpack he'd left there, a knock sounded heavily at the front door.

When they reached the smaller door that led to what had long ago been servants' quarters, he slung the pack over his shoulders, then eased the door open. The narrow strip of yard was empty, the path apparently clear to the small gate set in the rear wall.

They would be hidden from view of the driveway for probably twenty feet; the remainder of the distance to the gate, they would be visible to anyone looking from the direction of the car. Best scenario, all the car's occupants would be inside the house by then, none of them happening to look outside for a few seconds. More likely, someone remained at the car or had been sent to check the garage and the dorm, or both. Worst case, one of the men was already watching the gate, maybe from outside the property, out of sight until they burst into the alley, where his bike waited.

But, he acknowledged as footsteps shuffled in the front hall, they couldn't stay where they were.

He slid out the door, holding it until Cate had followed, then carefully eased it shut. Taking her hand again, he walked close to the house, listening to sounds of at least two, maybe three, men inside, straining to hear any noise from outside.

At the corner of the house, he glanced down. "Ready for a bit of fun, doc?"

Her knuckles white on the handle of her bag, she swallowed hard and nodded. With a nod of his own, they left the safety of cover and ran for the rusty gate. Short legs like hers couldn't run as fast as he could walk, but he kept a quick pace anyway, his hand on her upper arm half dragging, half carrying her along.

When they reached the open gate without incident, he released her and tossed her the extra helmet he always carried. "Put that on." He had his own helmet on in seconds, then used a bungee cord to fasten her bag to the backrest. She was still fumbling with the strap when he lifted her by the waist and hefted her onto the seat.

"Hey!"

"It's not brain surgery, doc, and we've got to get out of here."

He swung his leg through the space left for him and started the engine. Glancing back to see if she was settled, he caught movement in his peripheral vision, then a gunshot cracked in the heavy air. The bullet passed between them, exploding into a cinder block across the alley, and every muscle in Justin's body cramped.

Revving the powerful engine, he released the clutch and the bike shot forward. Zero to 150 in ten seconds, the manufacturer claimed, and he was pretty sure he'd just demonstrated it. He drove like a demon through four blocks of alleys, barely slowing before rocketing across the streets, then made a hard turn on the next cross street. It was a broad thoroughfare that didn't see much traffic, at least when he'd been on it, but it was also a risky place to speed, with police and military installations strung along its length.

His destination was a short distance ahead: one right turn, then another, onto a jammed street that passed cruise ships, dive shops and hotels. Their speed diminished significantly—down to ten, maybe fifteen miles an hour, with all the cars, scooters and tourists. His nerves humming, he kept an eye on the traffic both ahead and behind until he passed under the pedestrian bridge. Just past it, he goosed the engine, cutting it too close crossing lanes in front of a '70s-era VW Bug. He drove up the handicapped ramp, crossed the sidewalk and eased through an open gate.

A cinder-block wall sheltered them from the street. He nosed the bike in until the front wheel met the wall, then killed the engine and climbed off. He removed his helmet first, and he ran his fingers through his hair before grinning weakly. "Hell. This time I'm gonna kill Trent." He had to lean against the wall—his legs were that wobbly—and needed a couple deep breaths to fill his lungs again.

Cate finally swung her leg over and eased to the ground. She was steadier than he, but why shouldn't she be? She was an E.R. doctor. Life-and-death emergencies were part of her daily routine. Though not, he noted as her hands began to tremble, her own life or death. "Were those men police officers?"

"Doubtful. If it had been cops shooting at us, we never would have made it this far." Fairly certain his legs would hold him, he pushed away from the wall and unlashed her suitcase. "You have a swimsuit in there?"

She blinked, the only indication of her surprise at the change of subject. "Of course. Why?"

"Because we need to blend in, and in this part of town, most women are in swimsuits." He gestured broadly to make his point. "Put it on."

Her eyes widened with good old-fashioned modesty. *"Here?"*

He grinned. That might be fun—Cate Calloway stripping on a public street—but it wasn't gonna happen in his lifetime. "There are bathrooms down at the dive shop. Come on."

Both a ramp and stairs led to the dive shop doors. Divers were gathered around the dock, checking their equipment, and the shop employees were in and out, wheeling air tanks, answering questions, giving advice before the afternoon dive boat headed out. He wished he had his own gear and could just join the crowd. Under the sea seemed the last place those men would look for them.

Of course, the doc couldn't dive, but she wasn't his

responsibility. He'd be more than happy to pay whatever it cost to get her back to the airport and on the next flight out, or put her on a cruise ship for the remainder of her vacation. Anything to not have to deal with her.

But not dealing with her had never been that easy.

Once inside the shop, he pointed out the bathroom, then approached the man at the counter. Mario glanced up, then did a double take. "I didn't see your name down for this dive. How have you been?"

"Good, except I'm not diving this time. I'm here with a…friend who hasn't discovered the joys of scuba yet."

"She must be some…friend to keep you out of the water for long. Where is she? You got her hidden from the rest of us so we won't try to steal her away?"

"Bathroom. Listen, I just picked her up at the airport and was wondering if I could leave her stuff here while we have lunch."

Mario reached under the counter and produced a lock and a key. "Any empty basket you want."

"Thanks. Hey, and a T-shirt, too." Justin accepted the key, shrugged off his backpack, then pulled his shirt over his head, replacing it with the blue one Mario picked. Divers Do It Deeply, the slogan proclaimed above a picture of a smiling mermaid. After paying for it, he faced the dock. "You've got a good crowd."

"Regulars. Louisiana. Argentina. The single divers' group. You've probably gone out with all of them."

He probably had, which made him turn his attention back inside. He didn't want anyone besides the dive shop employees to recognize him. Keeping a low profile was something he'd had to learn, and he needed it now especially.

A couple of women came out of the bathroom wearing dive skins. They were solid women, in black Lycra that gave curves to their curves. Side by side, they completely blocked the view of the woman behind them until they angled off to the steps to the dock.

She was slender, shapely, nice breasts, well-defined biceps, flat middle. Her shirt was white, sheer cotton, unbuttoned to reveal a bikini top in the vivid colors of a vintage Hawaiian shirt: red, blue, purple, slashes of orange and yellow. A squishy straw hat covered her head, its floppy brim concealing her face, but there was nothing much hidden by her blue shorts—*short* being the important word. The faded denim clung to her hips and butt and left plenty of leg exposed, all the way down to a pair of flip-flops and painted red toenails. On an island filled with sexy women, she was one to make people look twice.

And she was headed to him.

Good God, it was Cate, looking less like a doctor than he'd ever seen her, and he'd known her long before she became one. She stopped beside him, one hand clenched around the handle of the suitcase she'd been pulling behind, and waited silently.

Mario gave a low whistle and grinned. "She might keep you out of the deep water, *amigo,* but be careful you don't wind up in hot water."

Justin's answering smile was more of a bared-teeth grimace. He was already in hot water. He just hoped Cate didn't make it boil.

Chapter 2

Cate protested leaving her suitcase in the locked wire basket at the dive shop. She didn't care if people stowed thousands of dollars' worth of gear there on a daily basis. The items in that bag were all she had on the island with her. The stethoscope tucked into her medical bag in the suitcase was the best for picking up subtle heart sounds; it had been a med school graduation gift from her parents, and she wasn't sure she could even hear anymore on lesser models. She didn't wear much makeup, but what she wore would cost an arm and a leg to replace, and her favorite well-broken-in sneakers were in there, too. So was her Kindle, and the sunblock that would keep her from self-combusting under the tropical sun.

"You can't go around dragging a suitcase without drawing attention," Justin said. He secured the lock, then hung the key on its cord over his neck and slid it under his shirt. "Have you eaten? I haven't eaten. Let's get some lunch. And a drink. Or three."

Scowling, Cate watched him saunter away before jogging to catch up. She grabbed his arm, slowing him enough to ease around in front of him and block his way at the base of the stairs. "Have you forgotten? Trent and Susanna have gone missing, La Casa is abandoned and someone shot at us!"

That one was still giving her palpitations at odd moments. She'd treated more than her share of gunshot wounds, but never, ever had she imagined that she could come *that* close to being the target of one herself. She'd *felt* the bullet pass her face, had felt the spray of dust as it bit into the concrete wall.

Justin was stubbornness in human form. "They're not missing. They're taking a break. They're relaxing somewhere, sleeping off a big lunch, and now *I* need a big lunch. If you want to fast until they get back, feel free. You can keep me company while I eat." Stepping around her, he started up the steep flight of stairs that led to the pedestrian bridge.

"Lazy, spoiled, self-centered," she mumbled, staying a few steps behind him.

They reached the bridge, and she broke off muttering. Ahead of them was a hotel, the grass lush-green, palm trees and flowers everywhere, the swimming pool glittering brightly next to a thatch-roofed restaurant. Behind them was the water, dotted with boats, the most amazing blue-green hue she'd ever seen. With the warm sun, the gentle breezes, the rustle of palm fronds and that incredible water, it was...

"Beautiful, isn't it?" Justin's voice was low and coming from right behind her, resonant, as it usually was, with self-satisfaction. But in this case, she couldn't hold it against him. "The mainland's over there. See those buildings? That's Playa del Carmen." He pointed, his forearm resting on her shoulder, bringing with it the mixed fragrances of sunshine and cologne. He smelled as expensive as he looked and, touristy T-shirt aside, he did look expensive.

And handsome, all golds and tans and browns, like some sort of tropical sun god.

She squeezed her eyes shut, chastising herself, blaming him. She wasn't a foolish romantic. She preferred substance over form. She'd had her heart broken once before by a man so exactly like him they could be twins, and she'd learned her lesson. She wouldn't repeat the past.

Besides, she didn't even like the man, nor he her, and she was taking a self-imposed break from *any* kind of relationship, even with men she did like.

"This isn't your first trip to Cozumel, is it?"

And *there* was a timely reminder of the man Justin Seavers was. "You know it isn't. Trent and I came here on our honeymoon. We stayed at a hotel down there—" she pointed to the right "—all the way at the tip of the island, and he had a fling with not one but two women who worked there. I'm sure he told you all about it when we got home."

For an instant, she thought she saw regret on his face, but his features shuttered so quickly, she was sure she must have been mistaken. He shifted away, then began walking again. She felt vaguely…guilty as she followed him.

On the opposite side of the bridge, a few steps led to the pool area, then a few steps more into the restaurant. It was open to the air, few walls, with an uncovered patio that held a scattering of tables. Justin headed in that direction, choosing a seat where he faced the ocean and the street.

"They've got great burgers here," he said, his voice level as the waiter brought chips, salsa and menus.

"I didn't come to Cozumel to eat a hamburger." She didn't realize how snippy she sounded until he replied.

"No, you came to find an outlet for that relentless do-gooder side of yours, to show people that you're more compassionate than they are and—" he accepted a bottle of water from the waiter and twisted the cap off before raising it in a toast "—to spend some quality time with your ex-husband."

Cate didn't know whether to be insulted, dumbfounded or amused as he swigged the water. She did have a do-gooder side. She wasn't nearly as giving as Susanna, but she donated her time and expertise when she could. She *wasn't* trying to put on a display of compassion. Most people back home in Copper Lake, Georgia, didn't have a clue about her volunteer activities, and she certainly didn't care whether strangers in another country were impressed with her. As for the last...

The sound that finally escaped was as much snort as laughter. "I gave up on quality time—*any* time—with Trent about five years before the divorce. In case you haven't noticed, he's in love with Susanna. In case you hadn't noticed, he hasn't been in love with me for years, if he ever was."

She'd thought he was, once upon a time. *He'd* thought he was. But Justin never had.

Uncomfortably, she drank some water while studying the menu. Everything sounded so good, including the hamburger he'd recommended, but by the time the waiter returned, she'd settled on seviche. Shrimp, fish and conch cooked by way of chemical reaction—there was a dish she couldn't find at home in Copper Lake.

Silence settled over the table after the waiter took their orders. She snacked on the chips and chunky salsa and watched the birds searching for treats on the patio. Justin watched the traffic on the street. To anyone who bothered to notice them, they probably looked like just another pair of tourists instead of two people who'd known each other thirteen years and had run out of civil things to say about ten minutes after they'd met.

Thirteen years. A long time. She'd been a sophomore at the University of Georgia at Athens. Justin and Trent had been juniors, despite the lack of attention they'd paid to their classes. College had been a four-year vacation for them, paid for by their families, with the only expectation that they earn a degree—not necessarily one they would use.

Expectations for after college had been slim, too. While Cate had studied her butt off in medical school, Trent had traveled—skiing in Colorado, cruising the Mediterranean, diving around the world—and Justin had gone with him. Her third and fourth years she'd spent days in clinical rotations and nights in the med school library, cramming data about each monthly specialty into her weary brain, and they'd gone mountain climbing in Nepal and surfing in Australia. Trent had barely made it back from China for her graduation, literally walking in the door of her apartment as she and her parents were walking out.

She was basking in self-pity, she realized, and that wasn't her style. So what if she'd begun her medical career with a grand total of $342,769 in debt? Who cared if they'd been out seeing the world while she'd worked so hard? She was a *doctor*. The only thing she'd ever wanted to do in her life.

Besides, Trent had paid off that debt as a divorce gift.

Yes, other husbands gave their wives wedding and anniversary gifts. Hers had rewarded her for putting up with him as long as she had.

"What did GayAnne tell you?"

Her gaze shifted to Justin, leaned back in his chair, wearing sunglasses that had come from nowhere. The backpack, she realized. He hadn't left it locked up at the dive shop with her suitcase. "Nothing. Just that everyone was gone and she was leaving, too. Where are they?"

His only response was a shrug so lazy, so arrogant, that she wanted to smack him. She curled her fingers around the water bottle to make it harder to reach across the table and do just that. "Knock it off, Justin. The volunteers have fled. The girls are gone. The local employees are gone. Susanna and Trent are gone. You know damn well they wouldn't just take off on a whim. La Casa is too important to Susanna, and she's too important to Trent. *Something* has happened, and you at least have an idea what or Trent wouldn't have told me to call you."

Another long swig of water, another lazy shrug. "Maybe he's trying to set us up together."

Cate sat back. The idea was ludicrous. As if Trent would wish her on his best friend, or vice versa. As if she would willingly stay five minutes in the room with Justin if she wasn't forced to. She didn't like him at all, but she liked him best when he was on another continent, and Trent was well aware of that.

She loaded her voice with scorn. "Come on, Justin. Tell me what the hell is going on so I can—"

His cell phone rang, and he raised one hand imperiously to stop her while he answered it. Rude, obnoxious, self-centered. She fumed as the waiter approached and set a plate in front of each of them. Immediately her stomach growled, overriding her annoyance. It had been a long time since breakfast, and she needed to refuel in order to deal with her present company.

The seviche looked incredible; the hamburger Justin had ordered smelled even more so. She dug in, closing her eyes briefly at the first mild, sweet, spicy, limey flavors, silencing the low *mmm* of satisfaction that hummed through her. If she'd been with her last serious boyfriend, AJ Decker—the cop who'd gone and fallen in love with his ex-partner while Cate wasn't looking— she would have immediately picked up another forkful and insisted he taste it. She didn't offer Justin anything.

Silence followed his *hello* for a moment, then his mouth tightened. The muscles in his fingers holding the phone contracted, too. He didn't look pleased.

Fear niggled in her belly, but it didn't slow her eating. She wasn't one of those people whose appetite came and went based on their emotions. Maybe it had to do with the pace of working in the E.R.; maybe it was a leftover from the frenetic medical school years, but when it was time to eat, she ate. She could do salvage work on a kid's leg dangling by a shred after a bicycle–pickup truck run-in, then go to the break room, wash up and eat a substantial meal of spaghetti and meatballs.

Besides, this call that displeased Justin could be about any number of things other than Trent and Susanna. Someone could have dinged his Ferrari back home in Alabama. A banking mistake could have temporarily delayed a payout from one of his multiple trust funds into his checking account. The housekeeper could have forgotten to vacuum backward out of his living room so she didn't leave footsteps behind.

Best friend or not, Trent was only a small part of the universe that revolved around Justin.

And *she* didn't register in that universe at all, except as a very minor nuisance. She'd learned that years ago and would never forget.

Bracing the phone between his ear and shoulder, Justin picked up the knife and cut the burger in half, then fished off the lettuce from one half. The call hadn't started off good: the caller ID screen had shown the number as unavailable. He rarely took those sorts of calls; with his money, his family and his reputation, there were way more people trying to contact him than he wanted to talk to. Under the circumstances, though…

The caller was a man, his voice heavily accented but easy to understand. *I saw you at La Casa para Nuestras Hijas, Mr. Seavers. I was warned you might be in the vicinity.*

Justin hadn't recognized any of the men in the black sedan, but why would he? He didn't generally hang out with thugs…though apparently he'd been somewhat friendly with men who hired thugs. How was it that he'd never heard even a hint of gossip about the seamier side of Joseph and Lucas Wallace's activities back in the States?

Because they hired discreet thugs, he thought grimly.

"What was in the backpack you took from La Casa?"

The man's question echoed in his head, and he worked to sound careless, more to impress Cate than the caller. He wanted rid of her, and the only way to do that was make her believe that everything was okay with Trent and Susanna. "Just stuff I need. You know, something to read, a change of clothes—things that don't fit in my pockets."

"You mean, things you took from La Casa. Things that don't belong to you. I want them."

Justin glanced at Cate and locked gazes with her. She was eating as if she didn't have a care in the world, but she was also watching him shrewdly. So far, she'd believed pretty much nothing that he'd told her, and this conversation was definitely going to make her doubt him even more and make her that much more of a problem. Sliding his chair back, he left the table and walked to the low wall that separated patio from driveway. There he couldn't smell the tantalizing burger or the seviche for the sweet heavy fragrance of yellow flowers that vined the wall.

His voice flat, he said, "Nothing in my pack belongs to you, either. What have you done with Trent and Susanna?"

"Mr. Calloway and Ms. Hunter are fine, for the moment. But that won't last if my employers don't recover the property Ms. Hunter took."

That damn flash drive. Susanna hadn't stolen the files contained on it entirely on her own. Justin had met her in the stairwell at the Wallaces' office building, taken the drive and disappeared while she returned to the offices for a meeting with Lucas.

"I don't know what you're talking about," Justin lied. "Maybe your boss just misplaced whatever he's missing, because I'm pretty sure Susanna would never take anything that wasn't hers. She's such a goody-goody."

"We've searched her, Mr. Calloway and La Casa. That leaves you. Any time Ms. Hunter has problems, she turns to you, and we know you were on the island that day."

Sensing movement behind him, Justin shifted. He half expected Cate, eavesdropping, but instead it was a tiny clubfooted bird, hopping around in search of tidbits. Cate still sat at the table, still eating, still watching him. Keeping her in his peripheral vision, he turned his gaze to the street, where one ancient VW Bug after another chugged past.

"What is it your boss thinks is missing? Susanna's taste is too good to pilfer any of that tacky art in the reception area, though I admit her purses are big enough to hide a piece. Or was it maybe something smaller? Did they leave a few grand in cash lying around that day? Or did it have sentimental value, like the gold lighter presented to Great-Grandfather Lucifer by President What's-His-Name a hundred years ago?"

His attitude was pissing off the man. It showed in the tightening of his voice. "Records," he said precisely. "She took records, and we want them back. Give them to us, and your friends will be released unharmed. Continue to hide the records, and they will pay the price. Call the authorities in your country or mine, and they will pay the price. Stand in our way, and you will pay the price. Do you know how my employers dealt with the last person who stole from them? Take a look at the photograph I just sent you."

Frowning, Justin watched the photo download, then his stomach heaved. It was difficult to say if the body lying on the sand was male or female, young or old. All he could say for sure was that he or she had spent some time in the ocean, the main course for a feeding frenzy among its residents. Please, God, after drowning first.

"By the way, Mr. Seavers, everything I've just told you applies to Dr. Calloway, as well."

"She doesn't know—" He broke off his automatic

denial. Damn! They'd been watching for her, too. The Wallaces must have known she was due back for one of her medical clinics. Whether they believed she knew anything was a moot point. She was here, and she'd been at La Casa. As far as the Wallaces were concerned, that meant she was involved. He could try putting her on an airplane back to Georgia or a cruise ship to nowhere, but she wouldn't be safe. As long as the Wallaces thought their business was in danger, so was Cate. He was stuck with her.

"Dr. Calloway doesn't have a clue about anything that happens outside her emergency room. Healthy, uninjured people don't interest her."

"Then if you both follow my instructions, her stay on the island should be quite uneventful. Now, do you know where the records are?"

Justin hesitated. If he lied and said no, the bastard wouldn't believe him. If he lied and said he had them, they'd want to set up an exchange, and he doubted seriously that the Wallaces intended to let any of them walk away from this. The fact that the man wasn't worried about any copies of the documents they might have made indicated that.

So he told a close version of the truth. "Not exactly. I've got some ideas."

"I suggest you start looking. I'll be in touch again soon. Oh, and Mr. Seavers—when you have the documents, don't bother making any copies. Keep your phone charged and nearby."

As the call ended, Justin stared across the street, where a cruise ship was making its way slowly to port. The Wallaces wanted the files back but weren't worried about copies. Why?

True, the files were encrypted, but Garcia, one of

his buddies in Mississippi, was working on that. She'd hacked into far better programs than any the Wallaces' tech guy could even conceive of.

So they wanted the information badly enough to kidnap Trent and Susanna—and to threaten Justin and Cate—but they didn't care about copies because the information was fluid. Names and locations could be changed. Move the people around and set their own hackers to erasing their existence...

Footsteps alerted him to Cate's movement in time to keep her voice from startling him. "Was that about Trent and Susanna?"

He gave her an irritated look. "Geez, you lock in on one subject and beat it till it's dead. No wonder Trent got so bored with you."

Her jaw tightened and hurt flashed through her eyes the instant before she pivoted to return to the table. Aw, damn. He hadn't meant—

He should apologize, but the Justin she knew didn't offer apologies easily—at least, not sincere ones. That didn't stop him from following her. She was rummaging in her purse for her cell phone when he reached the table. He tugged it from her grasp and slid it into his pocket with one hand as he picked up the bill with the other.

Stonily she stared at him. "Give me my phone. I'm going to call Trent's parents."

He did a quick conversion from pesos into dollars, then tossed down enough cash to cover the next three meals. "If Trent wanted Mom and Dad to know where he is, he would've told them."

Her gaze narrowed, making him feel like something small and slimy that she was about to dissect. She didn't argue, but turned toward the bar, no doubt to ask where she could find a phone.

He caught her arm and swung her back, half coaxing, half dragging her to the steps that led to the street. "You're tired. It's been a long day. Commercial flights are hell, aren't they? Let's go someplace quiet, and we can talk."

"Talk?" Her response reminded him of a parrot his frat brothers had inherited from a graduating senior. Whenever it was upset, it squawked like that. "I've been trying to talk since that awful moment at the house."

He grinned. "You mean when they shot at us?"

"I mean when I saw you standing in the doorway."

He flagged down a cab and ushered her into the backseat the instant the vehicle came to a stop. After giving the cabbie the address, he tried to casually glance around to see if anyone might have noticed them. He'd guessed not, but then, he hadn't exactly had experience with being followed.

As they pulled away from the curb, Cate straightened. "What about your motorcycle?"

"At the moment, I'd rather be in a car than on my bike."

"What about my suitcase?"

"We'll get it later. Don't worry. Mario will take care of it."

"But—my stethoscope—"

He rolled his eyes. "If anything happens to your precious stethoscope, I'll replace it. Scout's honor."

He wouldn't have thought it possible for her face to get any scrunchier, but she managed. "You were never a Scout, and you have no honor. If anything happens to my stethoscope, I will hunt you down and kill you."

Grinning was the last thing he wanted to do after that low blow, but he managed the brashest, most arrogant one ever. "Gotta get away from me before you can track me down." And that wasn't happening anytime soon, thanks to the Wallace brothers.

Bastards.

Despite her anxiety, Cate couldn't help but appreciate the scenery they passed: beautiful buildings, though set amidst some tackier ones, lush greenery and the water—that incredible-shades-of-blue water. Under better circumstances, and with better company, she would have her nose pressed to the window. More likely, she would instruct the cabdriver to pull over, pay the fare and head straight to the water's edge.

She glanced at Justin peripherally and gave a mental shudder. *Better company.* Oh, yeah, right.

The driver slowed and turned into a narrow driveway. Twenty feet in, he stopped at an elaborate wrought-iron gate, and Justin handed him a card to swipe.

The drive led into a very private haven dotted with palm trees and other vegetation whose names she couldn't guess. Bright waves of color competed against the too-pretty-to-be-real green of the grass, and the plantings hid any sign of neighboring houses.

The house that was the center of such beauty was a surprise. She'd never given any thought to what type of home suited Justin, other than the antebellum plantation that had been in his family for centuries, but this bare-concrete, industrial-type building that reminded her of Cold War scenes in Russia never would have made the list. It was so stark, so…ugly.

The cab stopped in front of a large black door, and Justin paid the driver before sliding out. "Come on," he said when she didn't move. "Welcome to La Casa Seavers."

Was he kidding? When he visited paradise, he lived in a squat, concrete bunker?

The moment the door closed behind her, the cabdriver accelerated away. She watched until he was out of sight, then turned back as Justin opened the front door.

Foolishness washed over her. Appearances were deceiving; hadn't she learned that along with every other little kid in the world? Plain and ugly on the outside, maybe, but breathtaking inside. One glance was enough to show that.

The floors were a mix of terra-cotta and aged wood, and the walls were painted in warm earth tones. The furniture looked comfortable, the art exquisite, and what she could see of the kitchen would make her friends who cooked swoon.

"Not quite what you expected there for a minute, is it?"

"It's lovely," she admitted. Then the bitchiness that seemed ever ready to pounce around him added, "Your decorator did a very nice job."

She wasn't sure, but she thought he mouthed the appropriate insult before he turned toward the stairs. Abruptly, he turned back and stared into the living room.

"What—"

"Stay there." He took the stairs two at a time, then disappeared down the hall.

Okay, she was a coward. She stayed, edging a bit closer to the door that still stood open. A few muffled sounds came from upstairs—not a scuffle or anything, just Justin doing whatever he was doing.

Her gaze went to the living room, trying to find what had caught his attention. A magazine lay on the floor next to the iron-and-stone coffee table, and one door on a heavily carved armoire stood ajar, less than an inch.

Two of the half-dozen pillows on the sofa were crooked, and one was upside down. Other than those small details, it looked more in order than her own living room had ever been.

Justin's steps thudded down the stairs, startling her. He reached past to close and lock the door, then started down the hall. "Come on. We're not staying here."

"Why?" She hurried to catch up, regretting that she had only a moment to register the formal dining room and that incredible kitchen before they were out the back door and on a patio that surrounded a sparkling blue pool. A block from the ocean and he had a pool?

The rich are different.

"Why are we leaving? Has someone been here? Why? Looking for us? And what does this have to do with Trent and Susanna?"

He stopped so suddenly that she ran into him. The backpack, at least half-empty before, now softened the collision. It still knocked the breath from her, though. It must have. It couldn't have anything to do with the fact that they were so close. She was way too damn old for that. Besides, this wasn't just any good-looking guy. It was *Justin,* for heaven's sake. Enemies since the day they'd met, remember?

He dragged his hand through his hair. "Okay, look, you're right. They didn't just go off. They're in trouble, and so are we. Yeah, those guys broke in here, looking for us and…"

"And?"

"And a flash drive with files that Susanna and I kind of, uh, stole."

Cate stared. She couldn't have been more surprised if he'd declared he was wildly in love with her. Susanna stealing… Oh, hell, *Justin* stealing… It was so wrong, not just morally or ethically or legally, but for who they *were*.

She didn't realize her mouth was gaping open until he pushed it shut with one fingertip under her chin. His grin was crooked. "I guess I should feel honored that you're stunned speechless. You don't think as badly of me as you like to pretend, do you?"

She tried to ignore the faint heat where his finger had been, tried to form a coherent thought. "So you guys st—" She couldn't say the word. "You took some data that belongs to someone else and they want it back so now Susanna and Trent are…what? In hiding?"

Grimly he shook his head.

Horror replaced that stunned feeling. "Kidnapped? They've been *kidnapped*?" At his nod, she shoved him with both hands on his chest. "And these same people were shooting at us and they broke into your house looking for us and— Oh, my God, what have you gotten me into?"

She shoved him again, knocking him back a few inches, and he grabbed her wrists. "Hey, it's not me. They got into trouble on their own. Well, more or less."

"What does that mean—'more or less'?"

"It means this isn't the time or the place to talk about it." He lifted her wrists a few inches. "If I let go, will you stop punching me?"

"Those weren't punches," she muttered. "I can show you a real punch." His grip loosened, and she jerked free. "I can't believe… Oh, of course I can believe it. You and Trent never did think about the consequences of anything you did. Why should you? Your parents or their money or their lawyers always took care of it for you."

Scowling, he took her arm and steered her toward the vine-covered fence at the back of the yard. "You're such a snot, Cate. When you see a patient in the E.R., don't you wait until you have his history before you start passing judgment?"

"I don't pass judgment. I treat their illnesses, patch up their injuries and turf them upstairs or out. My responsibility and interest end when they leave my department." Stolen information, kidnapping, getting shot at… Dear God, this was *not* what she expected of this trip.

He led the way straight to a gate that she wouldn't even have noticed, covered as it was with the same flowering vines as the fence. Brushing aside leaves, he typed a code into the keypad, then pushed the gate open and sneaked a look outside before he stepped out.

"So we're going to the police now, right? Or no, wait, we should probably call Trent's parents and let them contact the FBI. With all the lawyers and politicians in the Calloway family, they probably know someone who can get them straight through to the director himself, and we *are* in a foreign country. The FBI or the State Department should be involved. I can get in touch with Emilia…or maybe I'd better call Trent's dad instead. Emilia will be so devastated—"

Justin stopped short and faced her. "Stop babbling."

She stiffened. "I don't babble."

"We're not contacting the police or the Calloways or anyone else."

"We have to. We're not cops. We're not qualified to deal with a double kidnapping!" That was the way things went in her world: she came across evidence of child or spousal abuse, a sexual assault, a shooting, a stabbing, a beating, and she reported it to the police. End of her involvement, except for an occasional court appearance to testify.

"This may come as a surprise, doc, but the kidnappers—the people who have Trent and Susanna in custody, the people giving orders to the bad guys hunting for us—don't *want* the police involved. All they want is their files back, or they're going to kill them, and they're going to do their best to get you and me, too. I don't know about you, but I don't want to piss them off anymore than they already are."

She stared at him, his features as implacable as she'd ever seen them, then clamped her mouth shut and looked around for the first time since clearing the gate. They were on a narrow swath of grass, about as wide as the average car. On the left, fences and cinder-block walls marked the rear boundaries of homes and hotels that faced the ocean. On the right, heavy undergrowth that could conceal an army of thugs opened in a narrow gap to reveal the crumbled foundations of a structure long gone. Cozumel had found itself in the sights of numerous hurricanes over the years—probably the reason for the type of construction of Justin's mini-mansion.

He exhaled, drawing her attention back to him. He mistakenly took her silence for acceptance, but she wasn't convinced. "Did you listen to yourself just now?" she asked, the panicked tone gone from her voice, sounding much more like the seasoned E.R. doctor she really was. At least she had that much under control. "These criminals are threatening to *kill* Trent and Susanna. There's not even a question what we should do next."

"You're right. There's not. We're going to find a place to stay for a while and come up with a plan for getting them back. Come on." Shifting the backpack to his other shoulder, he started walking again.

Cate growled, surprising herself. Oh, she'd done it silently before when people annoyed her, but this was out loud, a good, threatening growl. She was that frustrated. But Justin's only response was a snort as he continued moving at a steady pace.

Even as she dogged his footsteps, she considered her options: call her ex-father-in-law anyway. Call AJ and ask his smart detective advice. Call the local authorities—

She couldn't call anyone unless she wheedled her phone back from Justin or managed to escape him long enough to find a pay phone. Wheedling was out—he would enjoy it too much and still refuse—and the idea of escaping him, of going out into town on her own when she didn't speak the language and every man she saw might be the one who shot at them, turned her insides morgue-cold.

"Unless you like playing the subservient little female scuttling along ten paces behind, you might as well come on up here where we can talk." Justin sounded entirely too easygoing. Why shouldn't he? He was a risk taker, an adventurer, a thrill seeker and, as she'd said, he never worried about consequences. He'd probably gotten an adrenaline kick out of getting shot at. He was probably looking forward to the next moment of danger.

But she was none of those things, and she just wanted the world she'd awakened in that morning to come back—the safe, settled, routine world.

She refused to jog to catch up, but after a dozen of the longest strides she could manage, she was beside him again. He looked so damn complacent that another growl nearly escaped before she forced it deeper down.

Despite his invitation to talk, he didn't say anything while they walked another few hundred yards. When she glanced over her shoulder, she couldn't pick out which grown-over fence was his, and she couldn't help but shudder as her gaze skimmed the opposite side. Anything could be hiding in there. Wild animals. Wilder people. The kind of people who were holding her ex-husband and her friend captive.

A shudder rippled through her, strong enough to make her stumble. Justin's fingers curled around her biceps, holding her upright until she caught her balance. She tried to put gratitude into her look, but it came off more a grimace than anything else. All the years they'd known each other, they'd never touched, not once, and suddenly he was grabbing her, pulling her, catching her, every time she moved, it seemed.

And she was grateful—for some of it, at least. Just grateful, nothing more, nothing less.

She was repeating that to herself when a car turned off the street ahead and onto the grass and stopped, facing them. The sun glinted off the windshield, hiding the occupants, and fear rushed through her veins. "Oh, God," she said breathlessly, her gaze darting around in search of the nearest cover. Another vine-draped fence was a few feet away on her left, the overgrowth more than eight feet to the right. The nearest cover was Justin, and she didn't hesitate to spin around behind him, her eyes closed, her hands clenched, waiting for shouted orders or a hail of bullets.

Instead, all she heard besides the thudding of her heart was…

Chapter 3

Laughter. Justin knew he shouldn't laugh. He understood that Cate was frightened. Hell, so was he, though not at this very moment. After all, he had called Mario for a ride while he was upstairs and told him what he knew about Trent and Susanna's trouble. It just wouldn't have been fair to ask him to involve his family otherwise. "Gee, thanks, doc. Let the bad guys shoot me first."

Her body went stiff and she opened one eye, then the other. Peering past him, she saw what he'd already seen—Mario's wife, Benita, standing beside a Beetle twice her age, her pregnant belly almost too big to fit behind the wheel, and four-year-old Rafael poking his head out the open driver's door. The tension drained from every part of Cate's body except her face and her right hand, still knotted in a fist. He quickly moved out of striking range.

She sniffed haughtily. "At least I know emergency medicine. If she'd shot you, I could put pressure on the wound until the ambulance arrived."

"You'd be surprised how much first aid I've learned over the years. I do care about the consequences sometimes." That comment had stung. Sure, he'd been a little reckless years ago, but who in their late teens/early twenties—besides Cate—hadn't been? He still took risks. Just living was a risk. A person couldn't exist in a vacuum—or, in her case, an emergency room.

But his risks were calculated. When he dove or climbed mountains or trekked into the wilderness, he was prepared. The experience was as safe as a man could make it.

Turning from Cate, he approached Benita and bent to accept a hug first from her, then Rafael. "Thanks for coming."

"I'm happy to help out." Her words had a faint, lyrical accent that hinted at time spent elsewhere. Before marrying Mario, she'd worked for a cruise line and traveled the world. She didn't seem to have any regrets that she stayed in the same place all the time now, spoiling a family instead of passengers.

Cate cleared her throat, and he stepped back to introduce them. The two women exchanged looks and nods before they all got into the car, Cate squeezing into the backseat with Rafael, Justin struggling to fit in the front passenger seat while Benita did the same on the other side. When she caught him frowning, she shook a warning finger his way. "Be grateful I didn't pick you up on the scooter. *That* would be a tight fit."

He'd seen entire families tootling around on bikes made for two. "Hey, I'm not complaining. I like Bugs. Love 'em."

Once the vehicle was moving, Benita shifted her gaze to Cate's in the rearview mirror. "I understand you're a doctor, you used to be married to Trent and you help out at La Casa."

"I am, I was, I do."

Benita's scoff was soft. "If Mario and I ever divorced, I would take him out on his boat, weight him down and send him to the bottom of the sea."

Justin grinned. "Yeah, but Mario's not like Trent. At least, not the Trent she divorced."

A glance over his shoulder caught a flicker of surprise crossing Cate's face. The instant her gaze connected with his, her eyes narrowed suspiciously. She didn't like him, didn't trust him, and he didn't care. Well, he cared only in that it would make the next however-many hours they were stuck together more difficult, as if dealing with bastards like the Wallaces wasn't difficult enough already.

But he didn't give a damn that she thought he was the same irresponsible trust-fund brat he'd been in college. It didn't bother him that she could overlook the same things in Trent that she considered fatal flaws in him. It didn't matter at all that she couldn't see past her prejudices or bother to notice that just like her, Trent and everyone else, he'd grown up.

He straightened and scowled out the front window. It really didn't matter, damn it.

"Where are we going?" Cate asked.

Benita glanced from the mirror to him to the street again. When he didn't volunteer an answer, she did. "A little place Mario picked out. No one will ever think to look for you there. I would never go there if my darling husband whom I dearly love hadn't told me to."

Justin grinned. No doubt, the hotel his dive buddy

had chosen was more than adequately substandard. The televisions, if there were any, would pick up only static; the mattresses would rate one thin level above the ratty carpet for cleanliness and quality; and the guests next door would likely be renting on a half-hourly basis. Back when he was young and foolish, he'd spent some time in such rat holes.

He'd bet his brand-new buoyancy compensator and dive computer, neither of which had even made it into the water yet, that Cate didn't know such rat holes existed. He didn't know whether to anticipate her discomfort or dread her whining.

Benita made a few turns practically on two wheels, quite an accomplishment for a vehicle as squat as the Beetle, drawing a delighted squeal from Rafael. The kid had pressed his back against the side of the car, his bony knees drawn to his chest, and was watching Cate with his head tilted to one side. Her presence kept him from his usual endless chatter.

"You can talk to him," Justin remarked.

Cate's gaze flashed his way, then she looked at Rafael and pitched her tone to a warm, cheery softness that she never showed Justin. "Hi. My name is Cate. What's yours?"

Rafael stared.

"You must be, what, about four years old? And you're going to have a new brother or sister. Which one do you want?"

Rafael still stared.

Without changing her voice at all, she spoke the next words to Justin. "Sure, I can talk to him. You just neglected to mention that he doesn't speak English, didn't you?"

"Aw, gee, and you don't speak Spanish, do you?

Sorry, doc, I thought you knew everything about the life in the universe." Suddenly pain shot through his upper arm. He jerked around the best he could in the confined space—which meant his head, neck and one arm were contorted around toward her while the rest of him continued to face forward—and scowled. "You pinched me." She'd reached through the narrow space between front seat and frame and *pinched* him.

"Stop fussing," Benita warned, "or I'll do it next time, and I leave bruises. Understand?"

Justin settled back. "I'm sure *she* left a bruise. I think I can feel a knot forming as we speak."

"Rafael speaks a little English, Cate," Benita went on. "But he's shy about using it with Americans. Rafi? What are we having?"

He smiled slowly at Cate before answering softly, "We are having a baby girl." Then his smile turned sour. "No boy."

Cate's smile came slowly, too, and was sympathetic. "No boy? Aw, maybe next time."

"Maybe," he echoed.

While they continued to smile at each other, Justin turned his attention to the neighborhoods they were passing through. He'd been coming to the island for fifteen years but had only a general grasp of the city's layout. He could locate the airport and the various hotels he'd stayed at before buying his house. He knew where every dive shop on the island was, along with his share of tourist-friendly clubs and restaurants. But Benita had made so many turns, and with each block the street seemed narrower, the buildings smaller and poorer, the people on the street tougher. This part of Coz definitely wasn't on the island tours.

Abruptly, Benita slowed to a stop in the middle of

the street and leaned forward to study the buildings on the right. Unpainted cinder blocks formed walls in front of and between the first three, one a store of some sort, the other two houses. A broken sign hanging crookedly from the fourth structure identified it as *otel*. She smiled with satisfaction and pulled into the narrow drive that passed into a courtyard. Nothing bigger than the Bug could have made it through without scraping the walls.

"This is—" There was a squeak in Cate's voice, and she tried to remove it with a deep breath. "This is where we're staying?"

Benita was still smiling. "It belongs to my husband's sister-in-law's cousin's father. They'll give you their best room, I promise. Wait here while I go inside."

He could see Cate trying to process exactly what "best room" translated to in a place like this. If the stubborn set of her jaw was anything to go by, she intended to make the best of it…which left him trying to figure out exactly what her best might be. As long as he was wondering, could he hope for cooperative? Maybe even quiet?

Benita returned a moment later with a key and wiggled into the driver's seat again. There was little room in the courtyard, but she maneuvered the car to the rear edge before stopping again and holding out the key. "Mario will bring dinner and Cate's suitcase when he gets off. Tio Pablo can provide decent beer and a fine bottle of tequila if you feel the need. When this is all done, you'll have to come for dinner again, right?"

"Right." Justin took the key, then unfolded himself from the seat. How had it been easier getting in than getting out? When he was standing straight, he shrugged to ease the tension in his shoulders while watching Cate climb out. She made it look so much more graceful:

one sandaled foot braced on the graveled drive, all the creamy skin of her leg, muscles flexing as she ducked her head and rose out of the car like a princess out of a battered rust-flecked pumpkin of a carriage.

She ducked to say goodbye to Rafael, then Benita. "Thank you for helping us."

"You're welcome." Then, with a grin, Benita added, "Good luck dealing with…" Her gaze shifted between them.

In unison he and Cate replied, "I'll need it."

Benita laughed as she shifted into gear and drove away.

The number on the key was faded, well-worn by years of sliding into and out of pockets and the lock. The corresponding room was ten feet down the courtyard, so he headed that way.

"Do you know I once did a medical mission on a remote, poverty-stricken reservation out west, and the place was cleaner and better kept than this?" she remarked as they sidestepped a trash bag that had been torn open on the scraggly grass, its contents scattered.

"No whining, Dr. Do-Good." He had to wiggle the key to get it into the lock, but it turned without too much effort and the door swung open. Surprised by the interior, he forgot to step inside. Cate got halfway around him before she stopped, too. After a moment, she went in, and after another moment, he followed her.

"Wow. I never would have thought…"

The room wasn't fancy by any means. It was so small the two beds were twins, with barely enough room to pass between them. Instead of cheap-motel bedspreads, they were made up with quilts, and a spotless vinyl floor took the place of cheap-motel carpet. The bathroom was a real bathroom—no sink and mirror against one wall, with a commode and shower in a tiny room—and it was spotless, too. The lone painting on the wall above the beds was an original of good quality, the lamps were bright enough to actually see, and the air-conditioning unit in the window lowered the temperature with no more than a quiet hum.

Justin made sure the door was locked, then set his backpack on the nearest bed. "It must be a family room, one they normally don't rent out."

The only response from Cate was the closing of the bathroom door. Grinning, he folded back the quilt on his bed, kicked off his shoes and stretched out on soft, faded sheets and comfortable pillows. Remembering the cell he'd taken from her and stuck in his pocket, he pulled it out, turned it to silent mode, then put it away again. If he didn't keep it close, the first time he dozed off she'd try to reclaim it and make those damn phone calls she'd been talking about.

Phone calls that *should* be made? She was right: they weren't qualified to deal with kidnappers. But he knew where the data the Wallace brothers wanted was, and he couldn't get that picture their thug had sent him out of his head. He didn't want to wind up that way, didn't want Trent or Susanna or even Cate to wind up that way.

He also knew more about the brothers than Cate did. Too bad he hadn't known more before he'd recommended Susanna's project to them for funding.

Cate came out of the bathroom, still wearing the same clothes, the same braid, but somehow looking fresh, as if she were just starting her day. Must be one of the benefits of being an E.R. doctor: deal with guts and blood and gore, and revive on breaks.

She'd removed the floppy hat—definitely a plus—and buttoned her shirt. That should be a plus, but he could see through the damn thing, and somehow having that thin, gauzy fabric just barely covering the bright colors of her bikini bra and the creamy gold of her middle seemed more interesting than safe.

She sat down on the other bed, facing him. "So." The word sounded momentous for one short syllable. "What's going on?"

There was a time to BS and a time to be honest. This, it appeared, was the time for honesty. Too bad. He enjoyed BS-ing her so much more.

He rolled into a sitting position, stuffed the pillows where bed met walls and leaned against them so he was facing her. "Okay. Do you know who Joseph and Lucas Wallace are?"

Her nose wrinkled, drawing her mouth into a dissatisfied set, too. "Trent used to call them Mississippi's version of the two of you. Rich, irresponsible, reckless, immature—"

"You could have stopped after 'you,'" he grumbled. "I got the picture. True enough. Except that the brothers inherited a chain of hotels right after college and found out they have an ability to make more money than they ever imagined. They own an interest in every top hotel or resort in the entire southern hemisphere, or so it seems."

"Trust-fund babies creating trust funds for their own babies. Who would have thought."

Her surprise honed the edge of his irritation. "You know, Trent and I don't jet around all the time figuring ways to deplete our trust funds even faster. We *do* stuff, too."

Cate took a moment to mimic him, pushing back the quilt, sliding off her shoes, banking pillows behind her for comfort. She might wish for that warm beer or fine tequila of Tio Pablo's, but she was truly comfortable for the first time since dawn. "What does Trent do besides help out at La Casa?"

"'Help out'? Is that all you think it is? He deals with all the fundraising. He brings in new money, and he updates the regular donors on what their donations are doing and keeps them happy enough to continue sending money. He does all the PR, arranges events for the girls and coordinates all the volunteers from the U.S. It's a full-time job for which he receives a room to sleep in and free meals, as long as he does some of the cooking or the cleaning."

Her first thought was to argue. That sounded like a do-gooder, which Trent certainly was not. *Doing good* was something he did for himself, not underprivileged kids in another country.

But he said he loved Susanna, and he said it with far more sincerity than he'd ever given Cate. People could change for love, could become better and kinder. She had to consider it was possible. Rather, she had to consider it might be permanent. She had to admit, every time she heard from him or Susanna, she expected it to be the time she heard that he'd gotten bored and said goodbye to Susanna, the school and the girls to return to his thrill-seeking, globe-trotting life. After all, he'd committed to *her,* and how long had it been before he'd left?

Could Susanna be different? Could the love he claimed for her be so much more substantive than the undying love he'd pledged to Cate? Could Susanna hold him when Cate couldn't? And would Cate mind if she did?

"Okay," she agreed. "Let's say Trent has transformed into Saint Trent of La Casa para Nuestras Hijas."

Justin's jaw tightened at her supposition, but she didn't let it stop her. His jaw had tightened, his brow had furrowed or his eyes had gone hard every time she'd ever seen him. It was part of the animosity that he usually managed to cover with sarcasm, faked good humor or mocking.

"What about you? What do you *do?*"

"I—" He stopped abruptly, and his expression turned totally blank. It wasn't as if he suddenly realized he had nothing to say, but as if he'd put up a wall instead. As if he had nothing he wanted to say to *her.*

The expression remained a moment before shifting into something sly, almost good-natured but not, almost relaxed but not. He moved into a more comfortable position, looking amazingly lazy and loose and, yes, damn it, handsome. "Let's see, in the past few years I've dived the ten best spots in the world. I trekked through the rain forest in southeast Asia and traveled the Amazon by canoe from the headwaters to the Atlantic. I spent last Christmas in Moscow and my birthday in the Gobi Desert. I hiked across Central America and had only a few run-ins with angry men with guns." His smile was the smuggest she could imagine. "Who knew money speaks every language?"

She stared at him, her back teeth hurting, but it wasn't the usual urge to smack the grin off his face. She'd already shoved him a couple times today and pinched him in the car. She, who never lost her temper, never lost control, who was so many years past pinching as a weapon, had pinched him. And she hadn't regretted it, either.

No, the pain in her back teeth wasn't as bad as normal because something seemed…off. Phony. The lazy, loose-limbed look. The recitation of his adventures. The smile. Maybe what he was saying was the truth, but not the whole truth. Maybe it was the only truth he wanted to share with her. Maybe...

He was a jerk and always had been to her. *Start the game the way you intend to play,* her grandfather the high-school football coach used to say, and Justin had started their association being a jerk. But if his dive-shop friend's behavior was anything to judge by, he didn't share her opinion. Neither did Benita or her little boy. She'd invited him to dinner—*again,* she'd said— and he'd agreed without hesitation.

Which proved what? That Cate was on his list of people who didn't deserve common courtesy?

She didn't like having people dislike her, especially based on superficialities. He'd taken one look at her the night they'd met and recognized that she wasn't like them. She didn't have money; she'd been wearing the uniform for the waitressing job that helped pay her tuition. She hadn't been sophisticated or witty, hadn't known a damn thing about diving or clothing designers or sports or booze. He'd dismissed her as unworthy two minutes after meeting her and had emphasized it at every subsequent meeting.

And she'd borne a hell of a lot of resentment toward him. Not just for trying to dissuade Trent from marrying her. Not for telling her the night before the wedding that she wasn't good enough for Trent. Not for dragging Trent off on a new adventure every time they were starting to settle in together.

She'd resented him because he'd made her feel *less.*

And judging by the knot in her stomach, she still did.

She hesitated to raise her hand to brush off Justin's list of vacations for fear it would tremble, but it didn't. "Okay, Trent truly does help Susanna run the shelter, and you do things that cost a lot of money and benefit you and the travel industry. Let's get back to the Wallace brothers. What do they have to do with Trent and Susanna?"

For a moment Justin looked as if he were wishing for the decent beer or fine tequila, too. He might even be throwing in a wish that he'd left her at La Casa for the men to do with what they would.

Then he sighed. "When Susanna started the shelter, she needed funding. The Wallaces give a ton of money to charity. Since they have offices here in Cozumel, I suggested they donate to La Casa. Give back to the community, you know. And they did."

"Why didn't you? Or Trent?"

His blue eyes darkened. "I don't know what Trent does with his money, and it's none of your business what I do with mine, unless you want to share your financials, too."

She snorted. Rich people had financials; she had a checking account and a savings account. He had investments; she had a retirement account. He had revenue; she got a paycheck.

And he was right that it was none of her business. She had better manners than that. She never pried into people's private business, except on the job, where knowing what really happened to a patient could mean the difference between living and dying. She did her best to minimize the risks of anybody dying in her E.R.

Besides, she knew how Justin spent his fortune: fun, fun and more fun.

"The Wallaces invest. They get a tax write-off. The shelter gets badly needed money. The partnership benefits everyone, and they're all happy…for a while. What happened to send you and Susanna into their office to take—" deliberately she rephrased "—to steal files from their computer?"

He ran his fingers through his hair, leaving a few blond strands standing on end. It gave him a look of boyishness that was seriously at odds with the definitely-not-a-boy body.

Not that she was noticing for any reason beyond a doctor's appreciation of anatomical perfection.

"After the first year or so went so well, the Wallaces decided to expand their involvement. They started an adoption agency here in Coz, working with a few of La Casa's sister shelters on the mainland, but primarily with La Casa. They did placements solely with American families, and they placed a lot of kids. Susanna was thrilled. She thought their success rate was so high because of all their contacts—family, friends, business."

The knot returned to Cate's stomach. Whatever was going on at the shelter, she'd kept it limited in her mind to Trent and Susanna. She hadn't let the thought that the girls might be involved even peek into her consciousness. There were so many ways to take advantage of children, of young girls with no families, who could disappear into the system so easily.

Justin's voice took on a darker tone, but his features stayed the same. Except for his eyes. The usual humor, charm—directed at others, never her—or irritation was gone, replaced by solid chunks of ice-blue anger. "A while back, six, maybe eight months ago, some women from Susanna's church in Idaho volunteered at the shelter. One of them really fell for a girl there, an eight-year-old named Luisa. The woman went home, talked to her husband, her pastor, the rest of her family, and they decided to start the adoption process.

"A few months later, the agency told Susanna Luisa's

adoption had gone through. They gave her a big going-
away party at La Casa, then kissed her goodbye the
next morning and handed her over to the social worker
who was going to escort her to her new family. Susanna
waited a few weeks, then she called the woman to find
out how Luisa was getting along, and the woman told
her—"

Breaking off, Justin rose from the bed and paced the
length of the room before returning and combing his hair
again. Cate was seriously tempted to plug her fingers in
her ears. She didn't want to hear what came next. But
she'd heard a lot of things on the job that she didn't want
to know. She kept her hands at her sides and waited.

"The woman said there must be some mistake. She
and her husband had been rejected by the agency. They'd
thought with the enthusiastic recommendation Susanna
had given, it would be a sure thing. It broke her heart
when they were turned down."

How hard had that been? Falling in love with a child
who needed you, in whose life you could make a real
difference, and being told you weren't good enough?
Cate wasn't particularly maternal—she got her mothering out at work—but it would have broken her heart.
"So Susanna spoke to the agency and they said…"

"The couple didn't qualify and Luisa had been placed
in another home. Naturally, they couldn't give out any
other information. Privacy issues, you know." He practically snarled the last words.

"Isn't it possible the agency did place Luisa in a good
home?"

He shot her a sharp look. "You think we haven't
hoped for that? Nearly two dozen kids had been placed
through that agency. Two dozen girls we thought were

happy and healthy and finally had a good home of their own forever."

Us. We. Those didn't sound like the word choices of a man who only got involved after the fact. Just how connected was he? Not to Trent, not to Susanna, but to La Casa itself? More than she'd given him credit for?

She would hate to have been that wrong about him. It would make her feel petty and judgmental, even though he'd given her plenty of reasons to judge him.

Deliberately, she refocused. "I'm guessing this nagged at Susanna's conscience until she had to know for sure where Luisa was."

He nodded and dropped onto the other bed, but he didn't sprawl back this time. Instead he sat directly in front of her, leaning forward, elbows resting on his thighs. Close enough that she could smell his cologne and see the faint variations of blue in his eyes. Close enough that she felt the need to sit back. She resisted. Just barely.

"She asked Joseph Wallace why the woman from Idaho was turned down, and he said he would find out and let her know. She asked a couple more times, and he brushed her off, saying he'd get back to her soon on that. So a week ago, when she had her regular monthly meeting with him, I flew down from Alabama. She went to the meeting early, sneaked into an empty office and copied all the files relating to the adoption agency and the shelter onto a flash drive. She passed it to me in the stairwell, then I headed straight back to the airport while she kept the appointment. We figured if they suspected anything at the time, they could search her or La Casa and wouldn't find anything. And any employees who might see me were a lot less likely to recognize me than Trent or someone from the shelter."

The idea of Susanna stealing anything still boggled Cate's mind. But if it was the only way she knew to prove that something was wrong, or to find out for sure what had happened to that little girl…

"Things seemed okay until yesterday. Trent went to pick up some donations from the Wallace Foundation, and he didn't come back. Most of the staff was already on vacation. Susanna called me, then sent the local employees away and had them take the remaining girls with them. She went looking for Trent, and she didn't come back, either." He exhaled and his shoulders rounded, as if the telling had worn him out.

"What was on the files?"

"Don't know yet. They were encrypted. One of my buddies back home is working on them."

Encrypted files, missing friends, young girls disappearing into the confidential control of a questionable adoption agency. And, oh, yeah, gunshots, a phoned-in threat and a break-in at Justin's house. Cold seeped into her bones, spreading until it made her shiver. She hugged her arms across her middle to fight the chill, but it didn't help.

She must have looked about as freaked out as she felt because, abruptly, Justin laid his hand on her knee, and he gave the closest to a charming smile she'd ever gotten from him. "Hey, don't worry. Remember you used to say Trent had the luck of the devil? He still does. He'll get out of this, and Susanna, too."

"When I said he had the luck of the devil, I was actually referring to you," she grumbled.

He grinned. "I know."

She tried very hard to not notice how long his fingers were, or that the tips were callused against her skin. He might live a life of luxury, but he didn't pamper himself. He'd earned every one of those calluses, and the muscles, with hard work. Too bad he didn't apply himself to something like a job or, just to be totally frivolous, making the world a better place, but at least he was dedicated to *something*.

As the moment of silence dragged out, she kept staring at his hand, its warmth slowly thawing the cold underneath. He looked relatively calm and reasonably assured, but she couldn't help but call to mind a take on a Kipling quote: *If you can keep your head when all about you are losing theirs...it's obvious you don't understand the situation.*

For Trent's and Susanna's sakes—hell, for her own sake—she prayed Justin did understand.

Chapter 4

"Tell me again why we aren't calling anyone."

Justin withdrew his hand—had she realized they'd touched more in a few hours than in thirteen years?—and hefted the backpack between his feet, unzipping it. "Because the bad guys with the guns and the hostages said not to or they would kill us all."

"So far you've talked about kidnapping and—" Cate breathed, but sounded fairly normal when she went on "—black-market adoptions at best, child trafficking at worst. Do you believe the brothers are capable of murder?"

"I do," he said flatly, as he dug through the clothes he'd stuffed into the bag to get to the cell phone charger near the bottom. He plugged it into the same outlet as the bedside lamp. The last thing he wanted—besides being involved in this mess—with Cate—was to let his cell go dead.

Just thinking the word *murder* made him wince. "That's a big step up."

He gave her a cynical glance. "Child trafficking compared to murder? They seem equally disgusting to me."

She nodded. Her little town might not be a bed of criminal activity, but it had some, and as an E.R. doctor, she must have seen her share of the violence humans could commit against other humans. "Isn't it fairly common for kidnappers to make threats they don't carry out?"

"I don't know. You'll have to ask your cop friends about that." Instantly he wished he could recall the words. No need for her to know that Trent had kept him updated on what was going on Cate's life; even less need to let her know that he'd paid attention.

She didn't seem to notice, but gazed at the drape-covered window and mused, "Making threats seems to me to be primarily a scare tactic to get people to do what you want. Actually carrying through on them—"

"They sent a photograph."

Her gaze jerked to him and sharpened. "Who did? Of what? Trent and Susanna?"

"The guy who called at lunch. And no, it wasn't them." He wasn't giving details of exactly what it was, and he damn sure wasn't showing her. She would just have to take his word for it. "It was a photo of the last person who stole from the Wallaces. Remember Benita's joke about dumping Mario at sea?" His attempt at a smile was sickly. "It's not funny when someone really does it."

Cate blanched. He half expected her to demand to see it anyway, to remind him that she was a doctor and had been dissecting dead people and putting back together live ones before she'd finished school.

She didn't, though. She just swallowed really hard and nodded. When she spoke again, it was softly, fearfully. "So what do we do?"

As he opened his mouth, a knock sounded at the door. She backpedaled across the bed so quickly that her head bumped the wall, and her eyes were wide enough to pop out of her head. "Damn, I wish you had a gun in that bag," she whispered.

"Me? I've never touched a gun in my life," he whispered back. He eased from the bed and went to the door. There was a peephole, but he kept thinking of the countless movies he'd seen where the victim looked out the hole and got a bullet through the eye in return. Stiffening his spine, he bent to look out.

An older man stood a few feet back from the door, a tray balanced in his hands. He was dark, his features distinctively Mayan, and he clenched an unlit cigar between his teeth. "*Señor, señorita,* I have refreshments."

He did: a couple bottles each of beer and water, three foam cartons and—bless him—a bottle of tequila and two glasses. Justin unlocked the door and opened it. The man smiled broadly as he carried the tray to the dresser. Turning, he acknowledged each of them. "I'm Pablo, and you are the friends of my son-in-law's cousin's brother-in-law, Mario." He must have caught the vague confusion on their faces. "We consider it all family."

"We appreciate your putting us up on such short notice," Justin said, the tequila on the tray damn near making his mouth water. What he wouldn't give to down the entire bottle, and maybe another one, if that was what it would take to pretend this day had never happened.

"Don't worry. As far as anyone knows but my family, you don't exist. If you need anything, knock on the door." Pablo gestured toward the connecting door opposite the bathroom. "Our quarters are next door, and my wife is always there."

"Thanks," Justin murmured as the man left again.

He reached for the tequila at the same time Cate reached for the foam boxes. Their hands bumped—nothing much, as contact went. If it had been anyone else, he wouldn't have even noticed, but this wasn't anyone else. It was Cate. Trent's ex-wife. The woman who raised every hostile instinct in his body. The woman who, in just the past few hours, had grabbed his arm, shoved him and pinched the hell out of him. His fingers should be itching to curl around her throat, not to touch her again. For damn sure not to see if her skin was as soft everywhere.

Scowling, he took the tequila and a glass and settled on the bed again. While he poured an unhealthy slug into the glass, she sat down and opened the boxes.

"Sandwiches," she said with disinterest. "Some sort of sweet." As he took the first long drink, she opened the third box. Her brows raised as she turned it around so he could see.

"It's a Mayan avocado. Is there lime? Salt?" He lost interest in the booze, surging to his feet, finding a dish of quartered limes and a saltshaker on the tray. "It's like a regular avocado, only about a thousand times better. They grow as big as your head—" He stopped squeezing in lime juice to cock his head and look at her. "Well, not your head, but anyone else's. They're incredible."

Her smile was as sour as the juice. "Oh, look, the egomaniac is insulting *my* ego. Isn't that—"

He picked up a chunk of the juiced and salted avocado and slid it into her mouth.

Her expression switched from sarcasm to bliss so quickly, it was comical. "Oh, wow."

She remained silent until the entire fruit was gone, when she licked the dribs of juice and salt from her fingertips. "That was wonderful."

"See? I'm right at least part of the time."

She opened her mouth, and he waited for her typical kind of retort. *Everyone gets lucky once in a while.* Or *When you waste your life partying, sooner or later you're sure to come across something good.* Instead, she just nodded. "I don't suppose I could stick a few of those in my suitcase on the way home."

"Not unless you want to hand them over to the customs guys."

His phone rang, a familiar tone, and he picked it up without glancing at the screen. "Hey, Garcia, give me some good news."

Amy Garcia was one of the few people, besides Susanna and Trent, whom he trusted without question. They'd met at the rehab center six years ago where he was recovering from a motorcycle accident and she was teaching computer skills to spine patients. She wasn't the least bit impressed by him or his money; she was blunt and honest; she had a tender heart, and she could sweet-talk a computer into dancing *Swan Lake* for her.

"I have a date tonight."

Good news for her, maybe. Not so much for Susanna and Trent. "Haven't you broken enough hearts?"

"There can never be enough men mooning over me, darlin'. How are things in your tropical paradise?"

"It's not looking much like paradise at the moment."

"Maybe I can change that. I accessed one of the files. I'm sending it to you as we speak."

Balancing the phone between his ear and shoulder, Justin put his drink on the night table, then dug the iPad out of his backpack. "Anything of interest on it?"

"Only if you consider the names and current addresses of every child adopted through the Wallaces' agency interesting."

He watched as the email opened on the screen, followed by Garcia's attachment. The database contained the girls' names, their adoptive parents' names, addresses and phone numbers, along with various dates and what appeared to be references to other files. "You're the best, Garcia. You should accept that job I offered you."

"Why? You get my services now for free. Besides, I like doing what I'm doing. I'll keep trying on the other files."

"Thanks. Did I tell you I love you?"

Her laugh was husky. "That's what all the guys say. Later."

After disconnecting, he gestured to Cate to join him on the bed. When she sat down, he caught a faint whiff of lime juice, underscored by sunscreen and, even fainter, cologne—something sweet and fruity. Hell, she smelled damn near good enough to—

Deliberately he blocked the thought. *Cate,* he reminded himself. The last woman in the world he was interested in. The last female in the universe he would get involved with.

He held the tablet where she could see the screen, too. "My buddy came through."

Twenty-two names scrolled down the screen. The youngest had been five at the time of adoption, the oldest eleven. Their alleged new homes were mostly clustered in the South, with six or eight scattered across Texas, Arizona and California.

Twenty-two girls who'd already been orphaned or abandoned, who'd already lived through too much hardship. Twenty-two girls who could possibly be living a normal life...or facing anything from slavery to sexual exploitation to death.

"All Susanna ever wanted to do was help girls like these. It was her dream. Her calling." He felt Cate's glance—so close; how could he not?—but he didn't look at her. He couldn't take his gaze from the names. "She just needed money, and the Wallaces had so much of it to give. She never imagined...*I* never imagined..."

Cate shook off the heavy silence that had settled over them. "Evil often hides behind good deeds. The Wallaces will pay for what they've done, and the girls... We'll find the girls. We'll make it right."

Then he did gaze at her. She wore an expression of fierce determination, the same look he remembered from the night before the wedding, when he'd told her she didn't deserve Trent. *He loves me,* she'd said icily. *We'll make it work.*

They hadn't. Trent had been no more interested in marriage than Justin had been. At the bachelor party, he had admitted as much, but it had been easier to go through with it than to disappoint his bride and his parents or upset all the elaborate plans. Back then, going along had always been easier for Trent, dealing with the fallout later. He figured there was no problem that wouldn't get better with time. Arguments would be forgotten, tempers would fade, a wife would undergo a total personality change and stop minding his absences...

Justin grimaced. Cate really had deserved better.

"Okay." Cate breathed deeply, sweet oxygen laced with expensive aftershave filling her lungs, then repeated, "Okay. We can't just sit here and wait for the Wallaces to call or for Trent's and Susanna's bodies to wash up on the beach somewhere." The thought made her shudder and a knot formed in her gut, but she doggedly went on. "We can at least try to find out what happened to these girls."

Justin glanced at her. "You want to go back to the States and…what? Ring some doorbells?"

"Why not? Let's look at what we know. One: Susanna asks questions about the adoption agency's policies and gets the brush-off. Two: she steals computer files regarding the agency and only the agency, right?"

He nodded.

"Three: she and Trent go missing. Four: people shoot at you and me just for being at the shelter. Five: you get a call threatening both of us, accompanied by a photo of the last person who pissed off the brothers." She gazed at the fingers she was holding in the air. Five small fingers, five big points. "If the adoptions were all legitimate, if they're just trying to recover stolen files, do you think they'd really use tactics like kidnapping, intimidation and threats of murder?"

Earlier he'd been trying to convince her the Wallaces were capable of murder, she reflected. It seemed he'd succeeded. It was the photo. She didn't need to see it. Just the look on Justin's face had been more than enough. If it had persuaded him the men were dead serious, she'd take his word for it.

"Okay. Where do we want to go?" He studied the database. "The best flight home would probably be Atlanta, and that would put us within reasonable driving distance of one, two, three…six girls."

"Then let's go to Atlanta."

He shifted the tablet, then began a search for flights. Her muscles taut, her stomach acidic, she stood to stretch her legs, walking back and forth the length of the room.

She wasn't used to being cooped up. At work she spent most of her shift on her feet, and with more people than she had ever wanted to see in a twelve-hour span.

She wasn't used to being scared, either. She *was* accustomed to worrying about Trent, though she'd gotten out of the habit since he'd met Susanna.

Since Justin had introduced him to Susanna.

"All right, we're on the 11:00 a.m. flight for tomorrow. You have anything in particular in mind for this?"

She turned to give him her friendliest smile and thickened her accent until it was heavy and sweet as honey. "'Hey there. My husband and I have just moved in down the street, and the neighbor said you have a daughter the same age as our little Lily, so I just wanted to come by and introduce myself and see if we could set up a play date. It's so hard for her, moving to a new neighborhood, you know.'"

Justin grinned and—who would have believed it?— it was charming. "Lily, huh?"

"'It's an old name in his family. I'm just grateful it wasn't Zinnia or Peony.'" She dropped the accent and picked up a bottle of water from the tray, twisting the cap off. "I assume the files are with Garcia." She also assumed Garcia was a woman. Justin just wasn't the type to say *I love you* to a male buddy. He and Trent had been best friends for years, and *moron* was about the fondest thing either of them said to the other. So when he called her a buddy, what exactly did that mean? Girlfriend, wannabe girlfriend, potential girlfriend, ex-girlfriend?

It didn't matter.

"Yeah, we'll swing by her place to pick up the flash drive in case we need it to try to make a trade."

It really didn't matter.

"Where is her place?"

"Jackson, Mississippi."

Cate could picture her: tall, willowy, blond—that was Justin's type. It had also been Trent's type before and after—and apparently even while he was with—her. She'd often wondered on lonely nights when Trent was elsewhere if coloring her hair would help keep him home more often. If she should work out enough to at least build muscles if she couldn't have curves. If she should dress better, wear more makeup, dumb down her conversation. But no matter what she did on the outside, she would never be tall, willowy or blond on the inside, so she'd stayed the drab little mouse and Trent had strayed further and further until their marriage was nothing but a sad joke.

Deliberately, she turned her thoughts to planning as she paced. Once they reached Atlanta, she would have to be the one to approach the parents. Justin was drop-dead gorgeous and prince of a powerful Southern family—just a tad memorable. She, on the other hand, was as everyday normal as they came. Ten minutes after talking to her, a stranger would have trouble recalling what color her hair was or whether she'd had an accent.

A queasy knot began forming in her gut. It always preceded major events—exams, the first time she'd ever examined a patient under the watchful eyes of her most difficult attending, the first emergency she'd handled, every true emergency, when the patient's life depended on her skills, calm and experience.

Her personal life wasn't exempt, either. She'd found no enjoyment in the ultra-fabulous dinner at the wedding rehearsal because of the elephants dancing in her stomach, and Justin's comment hadn't helped. The wedding was a blur of emotional highs underscored by dread. She didn't know if anyone else had seen it, but in their wedding portraits, there was a distinct hint of panic in her eyes.

Panic that was gaining a foothold in her stomach now.

"I have a couple of friends in Copper Lake who are cops." She hardly recognized her own voice for the breathiness. "And one of Trent's cousins is a GBI agent. We could talk to them, ask them to help, and the Wallaces would never know."

Justin stared at her a minute, his expression impossible to read, then turned back to the tablet. "They said no cops."

"But—"

"We've got nothing to bargain with, doc. They've got the hostages."

"We've got—or will have—the files."

"We've got names, addresses and phone numbers, all of which can be changed in no time. We have no proof these people or addresses even exist. We have no proof the girls are with them. For all we know, these kids could have been sent straight from Cozumel to Thailand or the Middle East or wherever."

He was right. Even if the addresses were legitimate, there was no way of knowing whether the children were still with those particular people. The parents on that list could have accepted the girls from the adoption agency and shipped them out the next day to places unknown.

"What if we find out that the adoptions are legit? That the church volunteer's bid to adopt Luisa was rejected because there was another set of parents on the list ahead of her? Or someone wanted a child so much that they were willing to pay a higher fee? Adopting children to the people able to pay most is immoral and wrong, but as long as the child is in a loving home…"

"If the adoptions are legit, why bother with kidnapping, attempted murder and threats?"

Her brow furrowed as she dropped heavily onto the bed. She could learn to hate that even, reasonable tone of his as much as she hated the smug, patronizing one. But, damn it, he was right. No matter what mysteries remained, that was one thing they knew for a fact: the Wallaces had something to hide within their organization. Something worth killing for. And it involved those little girls.

Her head throbbed, and the paravertebral muscles that ran along her spine were knotted. Back home she worked with an osteopathic doctor who could bring the most amazing relief with her hands—a few presses here, a few twists there, and Cate was ready for another twelve hours. She suspected Justin might be capable of some pretty amazing things, but nothing that would ease her pain.

Though he might make her forget it, a sly voice whispered, and wasn't that the next best thing?

"You look tired." Justin didn't sound sympathetic, exactly—more as if he were simply stating the obvious. "You might as well lie down. It'll be a while before Mario gets off and brings your stuff."

Lie down. And do what? There was no television and nothing to read except the internet on the tablet he was using. There wasn't even a radio to offer staticky music. The only option seemed to be sleep, and she was pretty sure she wasn't going to do that with Justin sprawled on the other bed.

She did lie down, though, settling on her back, knees bent, to flatten her spine. The muscles twinged, then slowly eased. "How did you meet Susanna?"

Justin glanced her way, but she kept her gaze focused

on the ceiling. She knew it was through him that Trent and Susanna had gotten together, and she really didn't care. Susanna seemed to do things for her ex that Cate never could—like make him want to be a better person. She was just curious how good-time Justin had met do-gooder Susanna.

"She lived in Mobile for a while."

She twisted her head to give him a chastening look, and the trapezius muscle in her neck tightened. "That's information, not an answer."

His features settled into a scowl, but there was no heat in it. "She worked at some community center in town with at-risk kids. My family gives a lot of money to kid charities."

That wasn't an answer, either. Since he was being evasive, he must have dated her for a while, though she wasn't tall, willowy or blond. She was pretty enough: average height, too curvy to be willowy, her hair too blue-black to ever be believably blond.

Apparently love, or serious lust, made physical appearance inconsequential.

Except in her case.

"Were you jealous when she took up with Trent?"

His snort seemed to take him by surprise, half choking him before he got it out. "Jealous? Remember— I introduced them."

"But not necessarily with the intent of Trent falling for her." After all, Trent had introduced Cate to Justin, but the last thing in the world he'd expected was for the two of them to hit it off. Instead, they'd only wanted to hit each other.

Justin laid the tablet aside and stretched out, piling both pillows under his head and facing her. "Susanna and I are friends. That's all we've ever been or ever will be. Trent and I were down here diving right before she opened La Casa. We went over to look around and to take her to lunch. She and Trent clicked, and I had to find another dive buddy for the rest of the week."

"Were you surprised that they clicked?"

"Hell, yeah. The only thing Trent had ever committed to was having a good time. He didn't exactly have any glowing successes in the relationship arena. Tons of ex-girlfriends, ex–one-night stands, ex-weeklong flings, an ex—"

He clamped his mouth shut so abruptly that Cate was surprised he didn't bite his tongue. "An ex-wife," she finished wryly. "With whom he broke his vows four days into the honeymoon."

"He regretted that. He knew he'd been a bastard."

She smiled at the ceiling. "So he did tell you about it." She'd suggested that earlier on the pedestrian bridge, but Justin's response had been to walk away without answering.

"I meant what I said at the rehearsal dinner. You didn't deserve him."

Yeah, yeah, heard it before, Cate's little voice responded, but it was silenced when he went on.

"Trent wasn't going to be a good husband. He wasn't ready for it. He was too immature and self-centered."

Her chest tightened, her lungs freezing midbreath. There were two ways to interpret *You don't deserve him.* One: you're not good enough. Two: you're not bad enough. Justin had always made it clear that she didn't fit in their world; she'd naturally assigned the first meaning to his remark that night.

But he hadn't meant that at all. He'd thought she'd deserved better than a husband who would lie to, cheat on and abandon her. He'd meant *better,* not *less.*

Wow. Justin Seavers had said something nice to her. Okay, so it had taken her nine years to figure it out, but… Wow. She would mark this day on the calendar.

People shot at me.

Bad guys threatened me.

And Justin paid me a compliment.

Even the worst day could have some saving grace.

It was an hour past dark when Mario knocked at the door, then hauled in Cate's suitcase, a bag of food from his favorite street vendor and a small cooler filled with water and sodas. He set everything aside, then took a seat at the foot of Justin's bed, smelling of sweat and ocean water and all things diving related. The scents were enough to make Justin regret the day of fun he could have had instead of dealing with La Casa's problems.

Problems which he'd contributed to by bringing the Wallaces into the picture in the first place. He owed it to Susanna and Trent to contribute to the solution now.

"So you're the doc I've heard so much about," Mario said, his gaze on Cate. His *interested* gaze, Justin noted, not that Mario would ever do anything but look. He knew about Benita's threat to feed him to the fish.

And why shouldn't he look interested? She was pretty and delicate yet still managed to give the sense that she could handle anything life threw at her. And she had those legs and those bare feet and those red painted toenails and that barely there bikini bra clearly visible through that hardly there shirt. Even Trent would give her a second look tonight, and he rarely gave her second looks even when he was married to her.

Idiot.

Justin wasn't sure whether that was directed to Trent or himself, because *he'd* been sneaking looks all day.

"I'm Cate Calloway." She leaned forward to shake hands with Mario. "Congratulations on the new daughter."

"Aw, Rafi wants to send her back already and she's not even here yet. He's convinced if he asks nicely, he can get a brother instead."

She chuckled, her face softening, the stress easing. "I tried that the last time my mother was pregnant. I wanted brothers so I'd have someone to do tomboy things with. Mom had twin girls instead, sandwiching me between four girly girls."

"You look pretty girly girl today," Justin teased.

"More womanly girl," Mario corrected, and succeeded in making her cheeks turn pink. He laughed, then turned to Justin. "What's the plan?"

"We're going to the States in the morning. See if we can find some leverage against the brothers."

"You hear about the body that washed ashore on the way to Punta Molas? They haven't identified him yet, but this family is convinced it's their son. He worked for a guy who worked for a guy… Eventually, it leads back to the Wallace Foundation."

Justin thought of the picture on his cell phone, and his gut tightened, a sour taste rising in his throat. He washed it down with a gulp of water from the bottle on the night table, then looked up to see Cate watching him sympathetically. She had probably seen something like that before; wasn't cutting up dead bodies part of her doctor training? She'd had her hands inside living bodies, touching things like hearts and kidneys and brains. One time, after visiting her at work on a very busy shift,

Trent had told him with real respect that she wasn't fazed by anything that came through the E.R. doors.

So she may have seen it. She could empathize with someone who never had. He hoped to God he never did again.

"Are you flying?" Mario asked. At Justin's nod, he said, "I've got the morning off. I'll pick you up."

"You don't need—"

"You know how small the airport is—six gates leading to one commercial runway. How hard will it be for the Wallaces to have people covering it?"

Cate's gaze met Justin's again, this time with a hint of fear. *Don't do that,* he wanted to warn her. *Don't look at me like I can protect you. I got Trent and Susanna and all those little girls into this mess. Don't count on me.*

"If someone's watching, we'll find another way."

"It's an island, man," Mario reminded him. "Planes and boats. That's it. If they're watching the airport, they're probably watching the ferries, too. Probably the cruise ships." He grinned. "But I doubt they're watching all the dive boats."

Justin grinned, too. "You get seasick, doc?"

"I don't know. I've never been on a boat."

"I have patches, and Justin's pretty good at holding people over the side while they puke," Mario said, referring to the antinausea patches that people never seemed to know they needed until they needed them. "I'm going home to my wife and child. Call me if anything changes. Otherwise, I'll see you about eight."

Mario let himself out, and the door locked automatically behind him. For a moment, Justin sat there, listening to the change in the silence, in the feel of the room. He'd been alone with Cate for the better part of the day, but it seemed different now. Maybe because it was night-time. Because soon one of them was going to go into the bathroom, shower, brush their teeth, get ready for bed. Because tonight he was going to share a bedroom with Cate Calloway.

The thought was unbelievable enough to make him smile. Real enough to tighten his gut.

She felt the difference, too—shifting awkwardly on the bed, looking anywhere but at him. When her gaze landed on the food, she jumped to her feet as if just waiting for an excuse, went to the dresser and began putting the bag's contents on the tray.

The aromas of warm pork and chicken, cilantro and corn, cheese and oil, permeated the room. There were soft tacos filled with meat so tender it fell apart. Warnings against street food in Mexico were legendary, but Justin had never encountered anything in Cozumel that he'd later wished he'd skipped. No food, at least.

They talked little while they ate. She asked about the food and the years he'd been coming to the island. As soon as she finished, she gathered her wrappers and napkins into a neat little ball, threw them away, then lifted her suitcase onto the bed. The zipper rasped loudly.

"I'm going to, uh, get ready for bed," she murmured, her back to him, bent at the waist to rummage in the bag.

She definitely had a nice butt. And for a woman who couldn't reach five foot five without stretching, her legs were definitely something. Trent used to complain that she wasn't athletic—no diving, skiing, mountain climbing, running, tennis, soccer—but either twelve hours a shift on her feet was athleticism enough to keep her looking damn good, or she had damn fine genes.

Justin couldn't resist looking past her to see the contents of the bag. He half expected to see it filled with scrubs—another of Trent's complaints—but what little he saw was far from utilitarian: lacy bras, tiny panties in eye-popping colors, slim T-shirts that would hug her snugly.

She straightened with her arms full, gave a vague smile in his direction, then went to the bathroom. To put that stuff down. To take off her clothes. To climb under the steamy, hard stream of the shower.

Justin closed his eyes. Could he be in a stranger situation than spending a night in a hotel with a woman he didn't like who didn't like him, either? Well, yeah. He could be sitting on his bed wondering what she looked like naked…felt like…smelled like. He could be getting just a little bit aroused as the sound of the water turning on came through the thin wall. He could be remembering that there was no lock on the bathroom door and thinking that conserving water by showering together sounded like an awfully good idea at the moment.

Frustrated, he popped his eyes open again. No, what he needed to remember was that this was *Cate Calloway.* The woman who'd taken a dislike to him the instant they'd met, who'd greeted him with disdain and an air of moral superiority every time after. The last woman in the world he should *ever* want to share anything with, besides a final farewell.

Before he finished brooding, the bathroom door opened again and Cate came out. Her brown hair was damp, slicked back, and gleamed in the light. Her face was shiny with cream, and her feet were encased in pink flip-flops so fuzzy that her toes practically disappeared beneath the fluff. In between were pajamas.

Of course she wasn't the type to sleep in a sexy little bit of silk and lace. He couldn't be that lucky…or God couldn't hate him that much. Depended on the viewpoint.

She wore cotton pants that ended just below her knees, bright pink with pairs of puckered streetwalker-red lips scattered all over. The matching pink shirt had one large pair of glossy lips in the center, surrounded by a slogan. *I'm a doctor. Let me kiss it and make it better.*

He was torn between offering her something to kiss and laughing out loud. The laughter won.

She shook a warning finger. "My niece got me these for my birthday. She's eight. All she knew was that I'm a doctor and she likes pink."

"Hey, I like 'em. You look cute." That was an understatement. Even in silly pajamas, the doc was sexy.

He yanked the stuff he needed out of his backpack and stood as she settled on the bed with a bottle of lotion. One shower coming up.

A very cold one.

Chapter 5

When Mario picked them up the next morning, Cate was relieved to see he was driving a minivan instead of the ancient Bug. She was about to pull out the handle to wheel her suitcase, but he took it from her, stowing it in the rear while she followed. He opened the door to the backseat for her, closed it after she slid inside, then went around to the driver's side while Justin got settled in front of her.

"Don't expect that sort of chivalry from me," Justin warned her, his amused gaze meeting hers in the rear-view mirror.

"You call common courtesy chivalry?" Her tone was about as unperky as she felt. She hadn't slept well. She would love to say that it was too much worry over her ex and her friend that had kept her awake, but she could at least be honest with herself. It had been Justin. More precisely, the knowledge that he was a few feet away in the other bed, wearing a pair of navy-and-green plaid boxers and nothing else.

They hadn't even been in the same bed, for heaven's sake. And it wasn't as if she'd never slept with a man before. Hello? The ex-husband, the boyfriends since then, including AJ Decker, whom she'd thought she would marry until she found out he was in love with a woman from his past.

But there was something intimate about sleeping in someone else's presence. Vulnerability. Forced trust. Potential.

Drums pounded a tempo in her head, stretching the muscles in her neck taut. She tilted her head first to one side, then the other, eyes closed until the blast of a horn far closer than a vehicle should be made her tense again.

"The goal when you drive in Coz," Justin said over his shoulder, "is to see how close you can come to the other drivers without actually making contact. Most locals are remarkably good at it. It's the tourists who have problems."

He was looking amused again, his mouth quirked in a restrained smile. Normally the humor he found in everything annoyed her, but this morning, there was something reassuring about it. Had he stopped being a jerk?

Or had she stopped assuming that everything he did was based on being a jerk?

They passed through neighborhoods, slowing at stop signs only long enough to gauge the distance and speed of oncoming vehicles. Before the trip was half over, she'd learned to keep her gaze turned out the side window, skimming over brightly painted buildings, squatty houses and overgrown courtyards.

She heaved a sigh of relief when they reached the airport. All those heavily armed men who'd practically sent her scampering back to the plane on her first trip would be a welcome sight this time. What fool would mess with Justin and her with all those policemen and soldiers around?

Abruptly Mario slowed down, and it wasn't for a speed zone sign; he ignored those the way everyone else did. "Over there. To the right of the terminal. Look familiar?"

Though there were cabs everywhere and travelers headed in and out, it was easy to spot the man he was talking about. He wore a Hawaiian shirt, untucked over denim shorts and at odds with the heavy scowl that flattened his features, and he was showing something—photographs, she would bet—to the policeman beside him.

"That's Guzman," Mario said. "Chief of security for the Wallaces, both at their offices and their house here."

"He was at La Casa," Justin added flatly.

"He's got company. By the terminal doors. Also down at the other end. I'd advise you to duck."

Cate's seat belt was half undone before Mario finished speaking. She slid to her knees on the floor, head tucked low. In the space between the front and back seats, she caught a glimpse of Justin. He was grinning.

"Bet no one ever shows you the town like this."

But the grin wasn't a very good one. It slipped and revealed a bit of worry behind it. It should have made her even less comfortable that he wasn't as confident as he pretended. Instead, she felt a little better. She didn't like being the only coward around.

"Now what do we do?" she whispered, as if the men fifty yards away could hear.

The answer came from Mario, his mouth barely moving. "Now Mario circles through the parking lot like he drives out here just for the pleasure, and then we forget about the friendly skies and see how the ferries are looking today."

Pain in her left leg made Cate shift to find a small plastic car beneath it. It made her think of Rafael and Benita and the danger. "Will the Wallaces suspect you of helping us?"

Both men chuckled. "I'm just a dive master," he replied. "I don't even own my boat. The Wallaces are…"

"Snobs," Justin said when he paused. "They give money to charity, but God forbid they actually deal with the people they're helping. There are so few people in Cozumel worthy of their friendship that they bring in guests from elsewhere for their events."

"And yet Susanna and I registered on their radar." Justin and Trent had already been on it, of course, coming from the same background. "I'm impressed."

"Yeah, well, I wish they'd never seen your faces or heard your names."

His voice rang with true regret. Cate was surprised and just a little warmed by it. Not that it was his fault he'd invited sharks into a goldfish-filled pool. People in his world were wealthy, yes; self-centered and experts on the concept of entitlement, sure; but mostly they weren't criminals. They didn't exploit children. They didn't fire employees by dumping them in the ocean to be the main course in a feeding frenzy.

And Justin had seen the results of that. Over the years she had inured herself to the blood-and-guts side of emergency medicine: missing limbs, disembowelments, the craters left behind by explosive bullets. He'd probably never seen a dead person who hadn't already been embalmed and made up for a funeral. It would take a long time for that image to leave his head.

It seemed they must have driven miles before Mario gave the okay to get up again. Cate scrambled into the seat, brushed bits of crumbs and sand from her legs, then refastened her seat belt. They were in a part of town she'd seen only once in recent years, when Susanna had taken her the long way to the shelter from the airport. Signs identified the street as Avenida Rafael E. Melgar, flanked on one side by the main shopping district, on the other by incredible blue water.

Mario turned left, circled the block, then came out on another street that faced the ferry dock. The pier was broad, busy with people coming and going, and had security near its entrance. Each of the armed men was standing with another man, and the other men, like at the airport, were holding photographs.

Silently, Mario made a quick turn, back the way they'd come.

"Are the police and the army here corrupt?" Cate asked.

"No more than anywhere else," Mario answered.

"The brothers are filthy rich." Justin twisted to face her. "Don't the police back home in Copper Lake pay special attention to any complaints from the much-respected Calloway family?"

"Maybe. Probably." She hated to admit it was true. The exploits of some of Trent's Calloway cousins were legendary, never resulting in jail time or any punishment their parents didn't dole out.

"Wasn't that why you kept the Calloway name when you guys broke up?"

Cate snorted. "Do you remember my maiden name? I had no desire to go through life as Dr. Proctor."

"Aw, then you could have specialized and been Dr. Proctor the proctologist."

She swatted Justin's shoulder, and he gave an exaggerated yelp.

"What is it with you? Were your fingers crossed behind your back when you took the oath to 'first, do no harm'?" He rubbed his shoulder, then his glare faded. "Okay... So, Mario, can you get us on a boat?"

Mario snorted. "I'm the dive master. Of course I can get you on a boat. I can't take you all the way to the coast, but if my cousin Pedro can meet us, he'll get you to Cancun and on a flight out from there. It'll have to be after lunch, though. The morning boats are long gone."

He turned off the main road again, heading north, or maybe east. Cate had no idea. The notion of getting out on the ocean appealed to her, though the fact that they were doing it to try to sneak out of the country didn't. Did the Wallaces' influence extend to the mainland? Could they use that influence to pick up a phone and stop her and Justin from getting on a plane?

If she got back to the United States in one piece and breathing, she wasn't leaving again.

They wound up at a tiny part-market part-diner for breakfast. She was apparently the only non-Spanish speaker in the place. Even Justin spoke fluently to the waitresses, more relatives of Mario. Frenchmen might claim theirs as the language of love, but Spanish, she decided, was the language of passion. Even ordering breakfast in it sounded exotic and fervent.

After the food arrived, Justin and Mario returned to English for her benefit. They planned and plotted, and she simply ate and nodded to everything. Mario would get them on one of the afternoon dive boats, and his cousin would meet them halfway between the coasts. Mario would provide a gear bag so they wouldn't arouse suspicion by dragging her suitcase and Justin's backpack on board the boat. He was also loaning them dive gear, his own and Benita's, so they would fit in with the rest of the passengers.

As if she could fit in with a bunch of divers. Trent had tried from the beginning to get her to learn, but when did she have time? She'd worked her way through college, busted her butt through medical school and a residency. The only vacation she'd taken in twelve years had been their honeymoon—not her best trip ever, considering her new husband had cheated on her twice.

But it wasn't her worst trip, either. This one held that honor. At least she hadn't *known* about the cheating until years later, while she'd seen and heard and *felt* the gunshot.

The rest of the morning passed too quickly. After breakfast, they went to Mario's house, a neat little cottage set inside cinder-block walls with decorative iron across the top. Little grass grew outside; most of the space had been converted to a lush garden, the colors so bright and intense that Cate was ashamed to compare them to her straggly little flower bed at home. Benita and Rafael were out visiting her mother, but she'd laid out the gear for Cate before she'd left.

Like the flowers outside, the dive skin was brightly, intensely colored and looked at least two sizes too small when Cate held it up. Noticing her skeptical gaze, Justin said, "They're supposed to fit snugly. Don't worry. They stretch."

"I know." She'd seen pictures of him and Trent in theirs. The garments stretched a lot and hid very little.

There were also a pair of booties, a mask, a buoyancy compensator, a snorkel, gloves and neon-yellow fins. Mario really wanted her to look the part. She'd be lucky if she could walk after she got it all on.

Far too quickly for her peace of mind, she was put to the test. After transferring all their stuff to the gear bag, a large rolling duffel, they drove to the dive shop. Justin's motorcycle sat where they'd left it the day before. As if prodded by the sight of it, he dug the keys from his pocket and tossed them to Mario. "Take care of it for me. And hey, I like the paint job the way it is."

Mario's only response was a wicked grin.

Inside the dive shop, he showed them to the cramped space that served as office and storeroom. Once he left again, Justin unzipped the bag, pulled out Cate's suitcase and opened it.

"Hey—" She bit off the protest as he removed her swimsuit. The pieces of fabric that had been perfectly adequate back home suddenly seemed so small in his big hands, especially the bottoms that he hadn't yet seen her in.

His leer was exaggerated as he examined the panty, the front and back connected by two thin strips of fabric decorated with bows. She *knew* she should have brought a maillot instead.

"Put that on, then I'll help you into the dive skin," he said, laying both pieces on the battered desk.

"I can do it myself, I'm sure."

"Okay. Then you can help me into my skin." Grinning, he turned his back.

"I can do this in the ladies' room."

"Or you can do it right here where I can keep an eye on you. Figuratively speaking, of course. I would never peek."

She stared mutinously at him, but he didn't sneak a look, didn't take his gaze off the large map that hung on the wall in front of him. Reluctantly she moved behind a stack of boxes that offered a semblance of privacy—from the waist down, at least—and hastily undressed.

"Do you know how many women I've seen naked?" he asked, his tone as normal as if they were talking about the weather.

"I'm sure more than I have, and I did an ob-gyn rotation." She dressed in record time but still felt inadequately covered. The temptation to pull her T-shirt back on was almost too much to bear, but damned if she'd let him know he made her that uncomfortable. "Besides," she went on with a flippancy she didn't feel, "you haven't seen *me* naked."

Whether it was her movement back toward the desk or some sixth sense that let him know when bare skin was covered—sort of—he turned, still grinning. "There's time, doc. As long as we're both breathing."

Flirting came as naturally to him as breathing. It was a good thing she wasn't susceptible to it. Or an incredibly handsome face. Or a grin that managed to be both wicked and innocent at the same time. Or a body that looked as if some sun god had come to life. Or…

Oh, hell.

He stripped off his shirt, then pulled out the two dive skins. "Time for the wet-suit wiggle."

He stepped into first one leg, then the other, tugging the Lycra up over his calves, and sweat beaded on her forehead. It was the room—small, cramped, warm with the day's humidity. After swiping her face, she picked up the second dive skin, balanced on the edge of the desk and did the same. The fabric did stretch miraculously, but she was damp, her skin sticky, and the suit didn't want to go on smoothly. She wiggled, wriggled, stretched and pulled, finally getting the material to her hips.

"You're not helping," he muttered, and turned his back to her once more.

Recalling his tease—*Then you can help me into my skin*—she sniffed. With the time and money to devote to diving as he had for half his life, he'd probably done this a thousand times. It came as naturally to him as scrubbing and gloving up did to her. The difference was, she was used to gloving just her hands, not her entire body.

Then he turned, just enough to give her a side view, and she realized what he meant about not helping. He was aroused. Not full-blown, all-out, would-do-Viagra-proud aroused, but on the way.

Heat scorched her from inside out. She would like to think it was shock, maybe even horror at the very idea, but there was that damn self-honesty again. To say nothing of the swelling of her nipples and the tingling in places she didn't want to think about, certainly not in conjunction with him.

Justin Seavers had gotten a hard-on watching her dress.

And she liked it.

Aw, hell.

By the time they were half-dressed in their dive skins and ready to join the other waiting divers outside, Justin had gone through every curse word he knew a dozen times in his head. What was he, sixteen again? He couldn't begin to count the number of times he'd watched women put on or take off their wet suits. Hell, even when he *was* sixteen, it hadn't turned him on, not once.

But those women weren't Cate, who was apparently some sort of witch who had discovered a great delight in not only irritating, annoying and patronizing him, but now also in giving him erections at the worst possible times.

Well, not exactly the worst. That would have been if they'd already hooked up with the Louisiana group that surrounded them. He'd dived with most of them before, and the guys never would have let him live it down.

They were gathered around the massage table underneath the straw-thatched *palapa,* waiting while Mario's crew loaded tanks and readied the boat. Justin stood with one hip braced on the table, while Cate sat beside him, looking as if she'd rather be anywhere else in the world. He didn't even take it personally this time. He would feel just as out of place dressed in scrubs and stuck in her E.R. with a bunch of people whose language he didn't speak.

Keeping half a mind on the conversation, he scanned the area every few moments. There was no one strange lurking around, no cars illegally parked on the street above, no one standing on the pedestrian bridge with binoculars for a better view. As Mario had said, the Wallaces' punks couldn't be watching *all* the dive boats. Still, that itch between his shoulder blades wasn't going to go away until they were on the boat and well away from the pier.

The call to board the boat couldn't have come soon enough. Cate trailed him to where they'd left their gear. Benita's BC, a bulky vest that secured the tank and helped the diver achieve neutral buoyancy, looked as if it weighed more than she did. Mario helped her onto the boat, with one of the other divers steadying her, and she moved to a corner at the rear. Justin was glad *he* hadn't had to help her.

And a little ticked that the others had beat him to it. He nodded toward the opposite end of the bench.

"Come forward, or the diesel fumes will get you. These guys prefer not to dive in water people have been puking into."

She moved to sit beside him, tension radiating from her in waves. The seasick patch Mario had provided was stuck behind her ear, and she stroked it from time to time as if making sure it hadn't come off. He had to give her credit. She was scared, but she still held herself together. A lot of women he knew would have had more than a few hysterics by now, but anyone looking at her would think she was nervous about her first ocean dive, nothing more.

Once the boat chugged away from the pier, Justin gave an inward sigh. Being out on the water always made everything better. He wished he had his own equipment, wished that instead of leaving the boat when they met Mario's cousin, he could go into the water with the other divers. The Palancar Reef was a beautiful place. Finning around down there for a half hour and photographing whatever sea life he came across was his favorite way to pass time. Cate would enjoy it, too. It was a whole different world from the E.R. where she spent most of her time.

Abruptly catching the drift of his own thoughts, he stiffened. Wanting to take Cate diving? Was he insane? Hadn't he figured out that she was a huge pain in the ass right after meeting her? Hadn't Trent and every other time he'd seen her confirmed it? She was the last thing he needed in his ocean, unless he was contemplating drowning her.

But she did look sexy in that dive skin, the devil inside him pointed out. And in that bikini. And even in those silly pajamas. Truth was, she was damn sexy. Period.

Staring at the tanks the crew had secured in the boat, he considered hooking up to one. Obviously, his brain was oxygen deprived at the moment.

Proving it, instead of getting as far away from her—from temptation—as he possibly could, he leaned closer. "You okay?"

Brushing a strand of hair from her face, she nodded, then asked, "You wish you were diving with them?"

He grinned. "Is it that obvious?"

Another nod. "What makes it so special?"

"Geez, ask a hard question, why don't you." He gazed over the water, at the cruise ships heading into Cozumel, the fishing and dive boats heading out, the ferries jetting across to Playa del Carmen. Finally he met her gaze. "It's...incredible. The fish, the water, the reefs, the freedom, the sense of discovery, the people. It's just you and your dive buddy in a whole new world. It's something everyone should try at least once. A lot of people aren't cut out for it, but you never know until you give it a shot."

Her nose wrinkled delicately. "It's dangerous."

"It can be, but, hell, doc, so is walking down the street. So is being in church if it's the wrong place, wrong time." He elbowed her lightly where the BC covered her ribs. "So is volunteering at a shelter for orphaned girls."

"You're such a cheerleader for it, maybe you should teach."

"I do sometimes." Seconds stretched out as he waited for her to ask for more. He wouldn't tell her everything, of course—that he paid for dive classes and trips for kids at the community center where he'd met Susanna, that despite Mobile's proximity to the coast, those trips were the first time most of the kids had ever seen the ocean, that it was one of the most fulfilling things in his life.

Her smile was touched with smugness. "Diving for Divas and Debs. Your students get to look good in their bikinis and dive skins, and you get…what? Your pick of the darlings?"

Part of every dive class was learning to deal with losing your mask. You went underwater and took it off, or your instructor took it off for you, and you had to put it back on and clear the water from it. After nearly twenty years, he still remembered that first time or two, the rush of water in his face, the fleeting but sinking sense of things gone wrong.

That was how the disappointment rushing over him now felt.

He didn't bother responding to her comment, but instead said flatly, "I'll be back." Mario obviously knew their plan, and the crew would do what he told them to, but the other divers would be curious when he and Cate left the boat, and curious people tended to talk. He wanted to give them a heads-up and a reason to keep their mouths shut.

And while he was doing that, maybe he'd learn to keep his mouth shut, too.

Cate had never been so exhausted in her life. Even attending med school classes all day and studying into the early hours of the morning or pulling twenty-four-hour shifts in the E.R. hadn't worn her down like this. Maybe it was because then, at least she was moving, talking to other people, keeping up a pace. Today she'd sat on Mario's boat; she'd sat on his cousin's boat; she'd sat at the Cancun airport waiting for their flight; she'd sat on the plane; she'd sat in the rental car, and Justin had said little to her. When he had bothered to speak, it had been the old Justin, the one who didn't take anything seriously. Especially her.

He'd cancelled the direct flight from Cozumel to Atlanta, then bought seats on the next flight to the U.S., sending them to Houston. Thankfully, for him, booking two last-minute seats had been no financial problem, even if first class had been the only choice. Of course, that was probably the only way he flew other than private jet. Wealth did have its advantages.

Now they were somewhere east of the city. She was too tired to know if they were still in Texas or had crossed into Louisiana at some point. All she knew was they were going to Jackson, Mississippi, and he wasn't wasting any time.

God, she was tired!

Justin glanced at her, his features shadowed by the dashboard lights. "You should have said something. We'll stop at the next town."

"I said that out loud, didn't I?" She managed a weak smile. "It's been a hell of a day."

The silence was so heavy that she thought he intended to go on not speaking to her, but then he sighed. "Two days."

This time the silence was hers, dragging on until she forced out the question she'd been avoiding. "Do you think they're all right?"

"Yeah."

Relief didn't even have time to bubble before he went on.

"For now."

"Do you think they'll survive this?"

His mouth tightened, and so did his fingers on the steering wheel, his knuckles turning white. "Not unless we find out what's really going on with the adoptions." As he exited the highway, he flashed her a sardonic smile. "Come on, doc. This isn't the first time you've had someone's life in your hands."

"It's the first time I've been responsible for someone I love."

He bypassed the first motel they came to, its No Vacancy sign flashing in the night, and turned into the parking lot of the next one. Stopping under the portico that covered the main entrance, he shut off the engine, then looked at her. "You still love him?"

The question surprised half a laugh from her. "Not in a bad way. Not 'ex-wife still in love with ex-husband.' Just as someone important in my life. Susanna, too."

He stared at her a moment, then got out and disappeared inside the motel. If she were a better student of human nature, she might think there had been a flash of something like relief in his eyes. But if she'd been a better student of human nature, she would have become a psychiatrist instead. Daytime hours, no blood, no guts.

Justin couldn't care less whether she was still in love with Trent, beyond knowing that it was hopeless. And thinking it was pathetic. Of course, he'd always thought she was deluded for ever believing Trent could love her.

He returned with a card key to a room on the back side of the hotel and surprised her when they got out of the rental by lifting the duffel out before she could even reach for it. "Don't expect me to always be chivalrous," he warned. "Next time it'll be your turn."

"Next time I'll be happy to."

She could get used to being in motel rooms with him, she decided as they settled in. The place was clean, a faint lemony scent in the air, and the beds were inviting. He dug through his backpack while she did the same with her suitcase. It was as comfortable as anything had been in the last two days.

"I'm showering in the morning," she said, clutching her pajamas and toiletries to her chest.

"Go ahead."

After changing into the pajamas, she scrubbed her face and brushed her teeth, then toddled back to the bed in her slippers. Justin was sprawled on the one closest to the door, fatigue etched on his face, eyes closed, so she pulled back the covers on the other. "I'm done."

His only response came a moment later: a small snore.

She considered waking him so he could undress, but she didn't. She considered wrapping the bedspread over him, but she didn't do that, either. After moving his backpack off the foot of the bed, she didn't do anything else besides shut off the lights and crawl into her own bed, drifting off almost immediately.

The insistent ring of a cell phone pulled her back to awareness. The room was dark, but the nightstand clock showed 7:06 and light seeped around the edges of the black-out curtains. She couldn't figure out why the ring sounded wrong until she realized it wasn't her phone. Who called anyone at 7:06 in the morning? she wondered grumpily, and Justin's voice, slurred and barely intelligible, suggested he was wondering the same. About the time he came wide awake, the answer occurred to her: kidnappers.

Scrubbing his free hand over his face, he sat up. "No, we don't have the files yet. I told you, I have some ideas. I need time to check them out."

He listened a moment, and so did she, straining to hear even the murmur of the man's voice. "If we wanted you to know where we were, we would have stayed at La

Casa or my house. But geez, your men broke into both places and shot at us when they saw us. It doesn't matter where we are at the moment. What matters is that we get the records back to you and you let our friends go."

Muscles knotted in Cate's gut. Sure, that was the trade the man had demanded, but it wasn't going to happen. Unless she and Justin found something—leverage, he'd called it—to use against the Wallace brothers, they were going to kill Trent and Susanna and then, because she and Justin knew too much, they would kill them, too.

She huddled deeper under the covers, her gaze locked on the bedside phone. While Justin slept last night, she should have called her ex-father-in-law, or AJ or the closest FBI office. Despite the Wallaces' warning, she should have asked for help.

And if it had gotten Trent and Susanna killed quicker? If it had gotten Justin killed? The Wallace family was far wealthier and likely more influential than the Calloways, probably more so than the Seaverses. They could have eyes and ears everywhere.

"Yeah, we'll expect another call." Justin's voice went dry. "We can't wait."

He hung up, started to stretch, then gave his clothes a look, as if he didn't remember he was wearing them. After scratching his head and leaving his hair on end, he finally focused on her. "You want the bathroom first?"

She shook her head.

Sliding from the covers—at some point in the night, he'd awakened enough to crawl under them—he gazed for a moment at the phone before looking at her again. "We're only a few hours from Jackson. Don't give me a reason to put you in the trunk for the rest of the trip."

Then, with a shrug, he said, "Aw, hell," unplugged the phone and took it to the bathroom with him.

She was certain she heard the click of the lock behind him.

Chapter 6

Jackson, Mississippi, home to half a million people in the metropolitan area, Jackson State University, the state capitol and Justin's good buddy Garcia, whom he didn't hesitate to say he loved. Cate had been anticipating meeting the woman since they'd left the motel this morning, but now that they stood at her front door, the elephants were back, tumbling in her stomach.

Why?

The first surprise had been the house. It was, except for its sunny yellow shade, the stereotypical middle-class house: big enough for two bedrooms, or three if they were small; a front porch with two rockers and pots of bright pansies; wind chimes hanging a few feet from a lush fern; a neat yard; a middle-class car parked in the driveway. It was very much like Cate's own house back in Copper Lake.

The second surprise was the woman who opened the

door. She was neither tall nor willowy, and only part of her curly hair was blond. Part was brown, and part was a delicate shade of peach. She was no taller than Cate, though much curvier thanks to the extra twenty pounds she carried, and she wore a stud in her nose, six or eight in each ear and a vivid-hued tattoo that snaked up from her left ring finger to disappear under her sleeve.

Cate expected her to greet Justin with a hug—after all, he'd told her he loved her—but instead she smacked him on the shoulder. "I've been worried sick about you guys. Why didn't you let me know you were coming here?"

"I have to keep my cell phone on for their next call, but I'm not using it." He rubbed his arm as if her blow had really hurt. "You don't want to find some guy on your doorstep with a big ugly gun wanting to know what you know."

She made a *pfft* sound. "Let 'em come. I've got the best security system in the state of Mississippi. Hardened steel doors. Bulletproof windows. A safe room that even the Navy SEALs couldn't break into...or out of," she added with a leer, "once I got them inside."

To Cate, Justin said, "Garcia's a little paranoid."

"Not paranoid, sweetheart. Prepared." She shifted her gaze—lavender, thanks to contacts—to Cate. "So you're Trent's ex-wife. Cate, is it? I'm Amy."

Cate accepted the hand she offered—a firm grip but not so much that the multiple rings Amy wore did any damage. She had never considered herself paranoid, but everyone knowing she was Trent's ex-wife was starting to wear on her. What had he and Justin told their buddies? Was she starting every introduction with big *X*s in the minus column?

"Want some coffee?" Amy asked. "Leftover doughnuts? A bathroom?"

"Yes." Cate never turned down caffeine, food or facilities.

"Bathroom's second door on the right. We'll be in the kitchen." Amy gestured toward the back of the house.

All the doors off the hallway were open, revealing a bedroom at the far end and two rooms converted to what looked like mission control: multiple computers, monitors, printers, bulletin boards, desks, phones. Whatever Amy did besides decrypt stolen files for friends, it looked far too technical for Cate's tastes.

When Cate left the bathroom and went into the kitchen, Amy was measuring cold bottled water into a coffeemaker that made Cate's little two-cup wonder look like something from the Stone Age. Justin pushed away from the counter where he was lounging and left the room for his chance at the bathroom.

"Isn't he a doll?"

Cate warily sat down at the small round table where three plates, a stack of napkins and a box of doughnuts had places of honor. "Justin?"

"I just love him to death. Being who and what he is— you know, *rich*—I never thought I'd like him, but after one day with him, I just adored him."

Confusion raised its pesky little head in Cate's mind. Who could possibly adore the Justin Seavers *she* knew after spending an entire day with him? His money, maybe, but him? And wasn't a lushly curved paranoid computer geek in middle-class suburbia just about the last person she would expect him to be best buds with?

Maybe Cate didn't know Justin as well as she'd thought. Maybe he'd grown up since those early days.

Maybe he'd changed from the entitled, self-centered jerk she'd known.

Maybe she was being judgmental and narrow-minded because maybe *she* hadn't grown up.

It was a disturbing thought.

"Where did you meet?" she asked, as the aroma of coffee brewing drifted into the air, rich enough to make her stomach growl.

"At the rehab center in Birmingham. I was teaching quadriplegic patients how to use computers to deal with their new limitations, and he was...well, rehabbing. After the accident."

Cate had heard of a number of accidents involving Justin. There had been the time he'd had trouble with gauges that had malfunctioned while diving and had run out of air sixty feet down. And the time he'd slid halfway down a mountain while ice climbing. *Those are the risks,* Trent had always said with a certain hint of relish. But she'd never heard anything about an accident serious enough to require rehab.

"The accident?" She tried to sound casual as she pinched off a bit of maple-glazed doughnut.

"Yeah, when he got T-boned on his motorcycle. They weren't sure he was ever going to be mobile again, but *he* knew. All those months, he worked harder than anyone there. I was impressed, and let me tell you, I don't impress easily."

"Who impressed you?"

Cate's gaze jerked to the doorway where Justin was standing, hands on his lean hips. He wore khaki shorts—it seemed that was all he'd packed—and a T-shirt advertising the world's best diving in the Philippines. He looked from Amy to her, then back again, waiting for an answer.

"You, my prince. I was just telling Cate how all the nurses at the rehab hospital fought over who got to help you bathe." She grinned at Cate. "A couple of them actually considered relocating to Mobile to volunteer at the community center when he—"

His forehead wrinkled and his eyes turned mutinous as he interrupted her. "You know we don't talk about that."

"Yeah, but this is Cate. Trent's ex-wife. She already knew." Amy's gaze darted to her. "You already knew, didn't you?"

Cate shook her head.

"Oh. Sorry. My bad. Mea culpa." A cajoling smile curved Amy's mouth as she snatched up an insulated coffee mug, filled it from the fresh pot and offered it to Justin. "Sumatra's best. Will you forgive me?"

His expression was slow to shift, and there was a grudging quality to it as he accepted the coffee, but after a deep sniff, he simply said, "Always," and walked over to sit across from Cate. His gaze, both arrogant and challenging, locked with hers.

She picked at the doughnut, nibbling pieces of crust with frosting. An accident had threatened to leave him paralyzed. And what was that about a community center? Hadn't she dragged out of him that he'd met Susanna at a community center in Mobile? If a couple of lovestruck nurses had considered volunteering there because of him, didn't that likely mean he had also been volunteering? This wasn't the Justin she knew. *Thought* she knew.

You're such a snot, he'd told her the day before, and it appeared he was right. Just as he'd pointed out to Benita that the Trent she'd divorced wasn't the same guy Benita knew, the Justin sitting across from her apparently wasn't the one she'd held a grudge against all these years.

And if that was the case, she felt foolish. Small. And with a lot to make up for.

When they left, Garcia hugged Cate, after trading email addresses with her, then smacked Justin on the arm again. "Stay out of trouble," she demanded. "And take care of Cate. Keep her safe. And Trent and Susanna."

He gave her a wry smile. "I'm doing my best."

"I'll keep working on those other files. Check your email."

He hugged her, and she clung a little tighter than she normally did before pushing back. "Go on now. Get to work. Find the bad guys. Bring yourself back home safe."

Noticing Cate's sour look as they walked to the car, he asked, "What's wrong? You don't like differing opinions?"

She slid into the passenger seat and buckled up before frowning at him. "Excuse me?"

He buckled up, too, then backed out of the driveway. "You have this image of me from college that you're determined to hold on to. You can excuse Trent for not agreeing, because we're so much alike, and Susanna because she's in love with Trent. But then there's Mario and Benita and now Garcia. You like them, and they like me, and you can't figure it out."

She didn't say anything for a mile or so, and when she did, the subject wasn't quite what he expected: "How could you keep injuries that severe so quiet?"

His mouth thinned. "It was an accident. Car ran a stop sign, hit a motorcycle. Who's interested in that?"

"An accident that made the doctors think you weren't going to walk again? An accident that happened to the media darling of the Seavers family? Don't tell me that's not worthy of a mention in the local news."

"My mother's secretary is a dragon when she's protecting her own. Besides, it wasn't that bad. The doctors needed a second opinion, and I gave it to them." He wasn't comfortable talking about it. It had happened a long time ago—he didn't even remember much of the first month—and he'd proven the doctors wrong.

So he gave her that cocky grin that usually made her teeth grind. "Let's get back to the fact that everyone loves me and you're wondering just how badly you've misjudged me."

She gave her own grin that was really just baring her teeth. "Nah, let's talk about how you interrupted Amy just when she'd mentioned the community center."

He followed the signs onto the interstate heading to Montgomery, his own teeth grinding. It wasn't a secret that he volunteered at the center, not really. His parents knew, and the closest of his friends. He wasn't embarrassed by it, though a lot of people he knew would be. You gave money to the poor; you didn't actually spend time with them.

But he didn't bring it up in conversation, either. It was his time, his business. If he'd wanted Cate to know, he could have told her yesterday or the day before. He didn't have to prove to her that he'd changed. If she couldn't figure it out on her own, too bad for her, because he *was* different.

After a time, he said, "Get that printout Garcia gave us, will you, and put the Montgomery address in the GPS."

She pulled the sheaf of papers from her purse, then

studied the screen, muttering, "I've never used a GPS. I always know where I'm going."

"Not this time, sweetheart," he replied. "If you did, you would've gotten off the ride a long time ago."

"Hey, you promised Amy you'd keep me safe."

He had, and he intended to keep his word. Somehow. Instead of reassuring her, though, he grumbled, "You know, there's something to be said for living life without others placing expectations on you."

Finally figuring out the screen, she entered the address, then sat back and sighed. "Sometime I'd like to try it. No responsibilities, no worries."

"No lives saved, no helping kids who need it."

"No getting shot at," she countered.

"Hey, I've been responsibility free most of my life, and that bullet came as close to me as you. There's no guarantees in life, doc."

Mouth set grimly, she shifted her gaze to the papers. Garcia had run every name and address in the file, comparing them to tax and utility records. All but three of the twenty-two families still lived at the addresses given, and she'd found new ones for those three. She was working more of her computer magic to get them background information on the family they were going to visit and would send it via email as soon as she had it.

While Cate was in the bathroom, Garcia had also given him the flash drive. Copies of the files were residing in the unbeatable security of her computer, but the original was in his pocket.

For whatever good it might do. The drive itself wasn't going to get Trent and Susanna, or him and Cate, out of trouble. Still, taking it had started this mess. Maybe, somehow, returning it would help end it.

In a good way, he hastily added.

"So...you work with kids."

He glanced at Cate, who looked remarkably good for the circumstances. Her hair was pulled back in a clip, her hands were steady as a rock and her face was smooth. Not lined with fear or exhaustion or frustration. Calm and in control.

"You're like a dog with a bone." A much better way to say she was stubborn than suggesting that her single-mindedness had bored Trent.

She met his gaze with a grin. "You'd have to compare me to a cat to insult me. I like dogs."

"Me, too."

"You ever intend to get married and have trust-fund babies of your own?"

The muscles in his jaw tightened at that hated phrase, but he let it go. "Get married, maybe. Have kids, no. There are enough kids already born who need a home. If I develop the need to be a father, I'll adopt some of them." After a moment, he asked, "What about you?"

"Get married, yes, if I meet the right guy. Have kids, no. I'm not exactly the mothering type. I like kids. I just don't feel the need to have one." She faked a shiver that set her ponytail swaying. "This is creepy. We've actually agreed on two things in a row."

He laughed. It was kind of comfortable, seeing eye to eye on something. Not that he would put it past her to take the opposing opinion just for the sake of argument. Not that he would put it past himself to do the same. He liked arguing, especially when it was so easy to push her buttons, to make her cheeks turn pink and her mouth get all prissy-prim and to watch her hair catch fire. *Don't poke the bear,* the saying went, but Cate was one bear who was damn fun to poke.

It was late afternoon when they reached Birming-

ham. While he followed the GPS directions to a neighborhood of grand old homes, Cate checked his tablet for
an email from Garcia. "Donald and Monette Clarence.
He's a lawyer, she runs her own advertising agency, no
other children. They moved into this house eight months
ago, just a few days before they adopted a nine-year-old
named Marisol."

He ran through the images in his head, trying to
place a girl with the name. He'd met dozens of kids at
La Casa, all little girls with dark hair and big dark eyes.
Some stayed only a few days, some for months. If he'd
met this particular girl, he couldn't recall her.

Marisol must have thought she'd hit the parent jack-
pot when she'd seen the big houses, the huge lawns, the
luxury cars parked in the driveways. The shelter was
probably the nicest place she'd ever lived, and the dorm
there was nothing fancy. He knew because he'd been
part of the remodeling crew.

He followed a gleaming black Lexus through the
neighborhood. It turned into a drive on the right as the
GPS's female voice intoned, "You have arrived at your
destination." Speaking of jackpots…

Turning in behind the car, Justin stopped far enough
back so the driver wouldn't feel trapped.

Cate's smile was nervous, but she was making a huge
effort to hold it steady so he pretended it was. "Keep
the engine running in case she releases the hounds. And
pretend to be on the phone in case she wants to meet
darling Lily's daddy." Then she popped out of the car,
pushing the door shut with her hip.

Monette Clarence was halfway up the sidewalk before she realized she had company. She stopped, then
backtracked a few feet to the driveway. Dressed conser-
vatively—black dress, red jacket, heels—she carried a

bulging attaché over one shoulder along with a smaller purse. Her hair, almost the shade of Cate's, was pulled back in a fierce braid, possibly the cause of her forbidding expression. But Justin wouldn't bet on it.

He did as Cate suggested, holding the cell to his ear, and rolled down the window to pick up their conversation.

"I'm sorry to bother you, especially just getting home from work." Cate doubled the sweet friendliness in her voice and emphasized her natural accent. "My husband and I have just moved in down the street—" she made a vague gesture to the south "—and our neighbor tells me you have a little girl about my Lily's age. She's almost nine. *Hated* moving after school started. You know how kids are. Anyway, I was hoping we could get Lily and your little girl together this weekend for a play date so she'd have a familiar face at school next week."

Monette radiated impatience and irritation, both showing in her cool, regal voice. "Your neighbor was wrong. My husband and I don't have any children." End of conversation. She dismissed Cate and continued to the house as if there'd been no interruption. She gave no sign she heard Cate's mumbled, "Sorry to have bothered you."

Barely opening the front door, Monette slipped through, with just enough clearance to give him a glimpse of an alarm control panel on the wall.

Cate slid into the passenger seat and buckled in as he backed out and headed out the way they'd come. "Okay, the backyard is privacy fenced, and there's a sign along the sidewalk for their alarm company. Unless we want to risk peeking in windows or climbing the fence, there's no way we can see if Marisol is there."

Steering one-handed, Justin traded his cell for a cheap

one from the console. It was a burn phone, a throwaway that couldn't be traced anywhere but to the store that had sold it. The only number Garcia had programmed into it was the number of her own burn phone. "Hey, Garcia, Mrs. Clarence claims they don't have any ki—"

Cate snatched the phone from him. "How good are you, Amy?"

He jerked it back and put it on speaker.

"So good I haven't been caught." The sound of knuckles rapping wood echoed.

"Can you get into the Clarences' insurance database? See if they have any claims to a pediatrician, maybe a dentist or a therapist? And what about school records? Can you find out if Marisol is enrolled in school here?"

"It would probably be a private school," Justin said. He heard the smirk in Garcia's answer: "Which only means it will take a minute longer, privileged boy. I'll call you guys back."

Cate disconnected, then folded her arms over her middle. "Could you see the way she looked at me? Like I was an annoying little bug trespassing in her universe. As much as I want these adoptions to be legitimate, the last thing any of those girls need is an ice queen like that for a mother. Hugging her would be like snuggling with an icicle." She shivered as if she felt the chill. "Now what do we do?"

Slowing to a stop at a red light, Justin glanced down the cross street. "I'm hungry. Are you hungry?"

For a moment she looked as if she might give a snarky response, then she rubbed her nose with one hand. "Yeah, I'm hungry, too." Before he could ask, she added, "You pick."

A mile down the street, he turned into a steak house parking lot. They passed a life-size bronze statue of a longhorn on their way inside, where a teenage girl in tiny denim shorts, a Stetson and cowboy boots seated them in a distant booth.

After they'd placed their orders and gotten their drinks, he asked, "Did you ever have to wear stupid uniforms when you waited tables?"

Cate's slow blink was owlish. Did she think he'd forgotten that was how she'd helped pay for college, or that he'd never known?

He hadn't forgotten anything.

"Only if you consider powder-blue polyester stupid, which I did." She folded her hands on the table, slender fingers, no rings, the nails neatly trimmed and unpolished. Spending her work hours touching other people and their bodily fluids, the last thing she wanted, he guessed, were nails that might tear her protective gloves.

But they were good hands. Steady. Capable. Certainly skilled at smacking him.

"What was the extent of your injuries in the accident?"

He gazed into his tea, wishing it was beer or something stronger. "You're the E.R. doc. You have an idea."

"Were you wearing a helmet?"

"I was. Put a dent in it the size of a softball." Though he couldn't feel less like grinning, he did. "Go ahead. Make a joke. 'How could they determine whether there was any brain damage? You were already an idiot.'"

She didn't smile. Her gaze didn't waver from his face.

"Look, it's not my favorite memory. In fact, it's not one of my memories at all. It happened. I woke up a week later. I rehabbed for a year or so. End of story."

He expected her to press the issue. Hadn't he commented repeatedly on her stubbornness? But she nodded. "Okay."

Before he could register more than brief surprise at her easy surrender, she smiled and said, "Tell me about the community center instead."

Cate waited while he unrolled silverware from the napkin, placing the cloth in his lap. He lined up the utensils exactly on the tabletop, then rested his elbows on the table, leaning toward her. It wasn't much—a good span of the table still separated them—but she swore she *felt* him invading her personal space.

"Why do you want to know?"

Several answers popped into her head. *Because you don't want me to.* Or *I'm having trouble seeing you as a kids' mentor.* Or *You make fun of me for being a do-gooder when you're one yourself.* She chose the truth. "I'm trying to figure you out."

That made him draw back an inch—a major retreat for the Justin she knew. Or didn't know, as the case seemed to be.

His smile wasn't quite as conceited as usual. "You've known me forever. What's to figure out?"

"Like you said, I've got this image of you from college. Trent's friend. The smug rich kid who didn't think I was good enough for his buddy."

His eyes widened and his jaw dropped, but she went on. "But Susanna, Mario, Benita and Amy see a totally different person. I'm...curious." Had he changed so much? Was he different with them than with her? Was she narrow-minded to think he was the same as thirteen years ago just because she was?

"I never said you weren't good enough. I never thought that. I just..." His mouth thinned, then he shrugged. "...didn't like you."

Closing her eyes, she raised one hand to her face.

"Hey, I'm sorry— I didn't mean—"

"No." Laughing, she lowered her hand again. "I didn't like you, either. You were arrogant and obnoxious."

"You thought you were better than me because you were smart and had a do-gooder goal."

"I never doubted you were smart. I just thought you were lazy and self-centered."

"I never doubted you were too good for Trent." His expression turned rueful. "When I said you didn't deserve him, you didn't think…?"

She nodded.

He winced. "No wonder you looked right through me at the wedding."

"It wasn't my happiest day. Me, my groom who had apparently passed second doubts and gone to fourth and fifth ones, and a thousand of his family's closest friends and business associates, 950 of whom I'd never met. Hell, I'd never met half my bridesmaids until the week of the wedding." Four sisters and a best friend hadn't been enough to satisfy Emilia Calloway and her wedding planners, so they'd chosen another five from Trent's cousins. "It was a spectacle."

"It was," Justin agreed. "And you were the most elegant, most stunning woman there."

Cate's stomach flipped. First he'd agreed with her twice in one day, and now he was complimenting her. *Elegant? Stunning?* Warmth crept into her cheeks and along her skin.

He was exaggerating, of course. There had been dozens of more beautiful women there, starting with his own date, the sort of woman who made men and women alike look twice.

"You have to say the bride is the prettiest one at the

wedding. It's a rule," she said as dismissively as she could manage.

"When have I ever followed the rules?"

"You do when you're diving. And mountain-climbing. And dealing with kidnappers. I, on the other hand, have never broken the rules."

"Obeying people with guns seems to make sense. I take calculated risks, not stupid ones."

Cate sighed wistfully. "I don't even take calculated risks, and yet here I am, in the same situation."

He stretched out his hand, curving his fingers over hers, and squeezed. "We'll find something to use against the Wallaces."

"Like what?"

"Proof of what their agency is really doing."

"How?"

"I don't know."

"Not a very reassuring answer." But she did feel better. There had to be *something* out there they could use against the brothers. Amy was good at ferreting out secrets on the computer, and Justin had the courage to go out and do the physical stuff. Cate? She was just along for the ride.

The waitress served their meals, the rich aromas of medium-rare beef, salt-encrusted baked potatoes, mushrooms sautéed in red wine and buttery, crusty bread making her forget everything else for the moment. "I love good food." The steak was so tender she could cut it with a fork, and she happily chewed and swallowed.

"You ever learn to do more than boil water?"

"No. I work twelve-hour shifts. I live alone. I can't really see the point."

"I live alone, too, but I cook." He broke a small, dark

loaf of bread open and tasted it. "I can do anything with seafood, and my bread is at least as good as this."

She eyed him as she ate another bite of steak. What little she'd seen of his kitchen in the Cold War house had been impressive, but she'd assumed it was there for looks or resale value. Surprisingly, though, she wasn't finding it hard to imagine him in it. "Where is home mostly these days?"

"Mobile. I still travel some, and I spend a lot of time in Cozumel, but mostly I'm home."

Volunteering at the community center. Being the older brother or father figure the kids never had. Maybe teaching them a little from his own mistakes with regard to the accident he'd been in.

Teaching... Yesterday on the boat, he'd said he taught dive classes sometimes. She'd made a smart-ass comment about divas and debs, and he'd walked away without responding. He'd hardly spoken to her for hours after that.

She'd insulted him, she realized—maybe even hurt his feelings a bit.

She speared a mushroom and savored it before cautiously remarking, "That's where you teach dive classes, isn't it? At the community center."

He stared at her so long she was sure she'd ticked him off by bringing it up again, then he shrugged.

"What's the matter, Justin?" she pressed. "Are you embarrassed that you're a do-gooder, too? Or are you afraid I might be impressed? After all, I may be clinging to the image of you from college, as you pointed out, but you have to admit, you haven't done anything to dispel that image. From the moment you walked into Susanna's office, you've been pushing my buttons just like old times."

"I like pushing your buttons," he replied with a wicked grin.

There was a difference to the grin this time, though. Two days ago, it would have made her want to smack him. Right now, she found it charming. Justin Seavers, who had never wasted one more breath than necessary on her, was charming her.

She tamped down the shiver trying to spread across her skin. "Just one straight answer, please."

He took a long time to meet her gaze, but finally he did, his dark eyes as serious as she'd seen them. "Yes. I teach the younger kids to swim, and when they're old enough, I teach them to dive. For everyone who works hard, studies and gets good grades, I arrange a dive trip a couple times a year. Is that straight enough?"

"It is. I'm impressed."

A slow, smug, sexy smile spread across his mouth. "I knew you would be."

She'd always believed she was immune to him—probably the only woman in the world who could claim that. Yes, he was handsome and sinfully sexy; yes, he had all that money. But she'd known what was beneath the surface. She'd been unaffected. Safe.

Heaven help her, she wasn't feeling very safe anymore.

Deliberately she steered the conversation back to the food and cooking, a topic that he warmed to almost as much as diving. She was pleasantly stuffed and had just put her fork down, pushing her plate away, when his cell phone rang. One of them, she amended. In addition to the throwaway Amy had given him and his own phone, he still had hers.

He pulled out the throwaway, hesitated, then handed

it to her. "You asked the questions. You take the answers."

Another wave of warmth fluttered over her skin at this slight gesture of trust as she accepted the phone. "Hey, Amy."

"Hey, doll. Dare I hope I'm disturbing something?"

Her cheeks heated another degree. "We're having dinner."

"Ah. Eat a bite for me, will you? Listen, I did the checking you asked. Really, the Clarences' insurance company needs better security. For that matter, so does the school district there. There have been no visits, on the record at least, to a pediatrician, and the only payouts on their dental insurance have been for semiannual checkups for him and her. Also, the only therapist is hers, at $250 an hour. You make that kind of money?"

Cate scoffed. She was well paid, but not *that* well paid.

"Me neither. They don't have any little Clarences enrolled in the public school system. Don't tell Justin this, but it was taking longer to check the private schools than I expected, so I pulled their financial records instead. No tuition being paid out to a private school. No babysitter or nanny or housekeeper to watch the kiddo while Mom and Dad are at work. No expenditures at Toys'R'Us or for piano lessons or ballet or gymnastics or anything along those lines. In other words, nothing to suggest that they have a child *except* for a charitable donation of $150,000 to the Wallace Foundation eight months ago."

Cate's fingers tightened until the tips went numb. The Clarences could have adopted an older child here in the U.S. for far less than that amount, if a child was all they wanted. Of course, there were background checks, evaluations and home visits to go through here, not the sham of a process the Wallaces used, and any child who was placed could be taken away for cause.

Amy was thinking along the same lines. "Older kids are a dime a dozen in the adoption system in the U.S., which begs the question: What exactly did they want with the girl that they paid so much money?" Immediately she pleaded, "Oh, God, don't answer that. I have too many ideas in my head already, and they're all horrible. Those bastards."

The Clarences wanted to keep Marisol off the radar. They didn't want anyone in Montgomery to know she existed. They wanted the freedom to do anything, anytime, with no consequences.

Cate's stomach knotted, and she thought for one moment that she might have to make a run for the bathroom to heave up that delicious dinner. A few deep breaths, along with the cold anger building inside, settled it, though. "Where is the next closest family?"

A few clicks of the keyboard sounded in the background, then Amy said, "Looks like a toss-up between Atlanta and Decatur, Alabama. Want me to start on those families?"

"Yes, please. We'll let you know where we're headed when we know."

"Okay. Hold it together, sweetie."

I'll try. Cate gave the phone back to Justin, slid from the booth and walked out of the restaurant. The night air was cool, muggy, filled with the sounds of traffic and music thumping from a nearby club. Hugging herself, she paced to the longhorn statue, then leaned against it and stared at the sky. Was Marisol seeing those stars? Was she still in Alabama? Was she even still alive? And if she was, in what condition? What had she endured?

A sob almost escaped, but she choked it back. Maybe they were wrong. Maybe Marisol was in a happy, loving home, and there were no doctor visits because she was healthy and strong, and there were no school records or babysitting expenses because she was being homeschooled by an adoring aunt or grandmother who lived nearby. Maybe she was the treasure of her new little family and life was better than she'd ever imagined it might be.

Right. Maybe all twenty-two girls were happy and healthy, and maybe the Wallaces would release Trent and Susanna with an apology, sign all their assets over to La Casa, then turn themselves in to the authorities for their crimes.

Footsteps sounded on the pavement, but she didn't look up, not even when strong arms slid around her from behind. "It's going to be okay," Justin murmured, his mouth brushing her ear. "I swear, we'll make it right."

She'd told him the same thing in the motel the first day, and at the time, she'd believed it. Had he found the words any more reassuring then than she did now? Gripping his wrists with both hands, she shifted her weight until he was supporting her rather than the statue. "Can it be made right? Those little girls…all they've been through…"

She didn't go on. As Amy had said, she had too many ideas in her head, and they were all horrible.

"How's this— We'll do our best, and we'll make damn sure the Wallaces and everyone else involved pay dearly for what they've done. Deal?"

She clung a little tighter, as if intensity could make it so, and whispered in return, "Deal."

Chapter 7

They stood there a long time, next to a damn cow statue in a parking lot in the middle of Montgomery, before Justin broke the silence. "I called Garcia. She told me everything."

The tension that had finally left Cate's body rushed back. It was sharp and tingling every place they were in contact, and that was a hell of a lot of places. He reminded himself that *that* was why he was holding her, because she'd been obviously upset. It wasn't supposed to feel good, not with Cate.

But it did. Damn good.

The pressure of her hands on his eased, then she twisted out of his arms and backed away a few steps, arms folded again. Was the gesture habit? Body language for *Don't touch me?* Or was she unused to having someone hold her?

"We should go," she said, avoiding his gaze.

"We should stop for the night."

"I'm not tired."

"I am." And she was, too. It showed in the lines around her mouth, in the shadows of her eyes. It had been a tough couple of days, even for a competent E.R. doctor who was used to running on adrenaline. This was an entirely different kind of stress. "We'll find a room, get a good night's sleep and head to Atlanta in the morning. There are three families there. By the time we finish breakfast, Garcia will have everything we need to know."

Her nod wasn't convincing, but it was agreement.

They walked to the car together, where she finally looked at him. "I'm sorry I ran out like that."

He forced a grin that he didn't feel. He was good at it. "Aw, you're just sorry that you pushed me away. The idea throws you for a loop, doesn't it, doc? You and me working together. Being friends. Maybe more."

She summoned a scowl that he suspected she didn't quite feel, either. "'Maybe more'?" she echoed as she slid into the car. "You wish." The slamming door emphasized the retort.

"I do," he murmured, surprising himself, then rolled his eyes skyward. More? With *Cate?* But reminding himself who she was didn't have the same effect it used to. Yeah, he'd disliked her in college, but as she'd pointed out, he'd been a jerk then, too. If he put those years out of his mind and concentrated solely on who she was now… He liked this Cate. A lot. Maybe enough to want *something* with her.

Maybe it was just chemistry. The lingering image of her struggling into the dive skin yesterday. The adrenaline rush of dangerous circumstances. Sharing a room with her sleeping in those sexy, silly pajamas. Listening while she showered. Seeing her vulnerable and scared and determined to stand and fight.

He liked her. Admired her. He didn't totally trust her, he acknowledged, thinking of the collection of cells in his pockets. But he wanted her. The hard-on he'd gotten watching her struggle into the dive skin was proof of that.

Hell.

When he got into the car, he used the GPS to find a motel near the interstate that would take them to Atlanta in the morning. The room was clean, spacious, newly renovated according to the sign in the lobby, and the air smelled subtly of vanilla, cool and welcoming. When he put the bags on the two beds, he remarked, "It lacks the charm of Tio Pablo's place, doesn't it?"

Cate's laugh was the closest to worry-free emotion she'd shown in the past few hours. "You're missing the charm of the tequila and the Mayan avocado." She faked a wistful sigh. "An avocado would be awfully good right now."

They each sat on their own beds and reached for their bags. She unzipped her suitcase and carefully removed everything she needed for the night. It was packed as neatly right now as it had been when she'd left Copper Lake. A zippered vinyl bag on top held her laundry; her house shoes were packed in a smaller version; toiletries in leakproof bags filled in the spaces between folded clothing; and her medical bag was securely tucked in the bottom.

His backpack, on the other hand, was a mess. He dumped it out: a plastic trash bag from Tio Pablo's that held his dirty clothes; four loose socks, a pair of brown shorts, a T-shirt and a pair of boxers; a razor, toothbrush, toothpaste and cologne stuffed into a small inner pocket.

His tablet and a file folder tumbled out, too, along with chargers for the tablet and the cell.

"What's in the folder?"

He handed it over, and she pulled out a sheaf of papers. The top one was a photograph of Susanna and Trent, standing in the yard in front of La Casa. Underneath was a sheet with their parents' names, addresses and their phone numbers. The rest were snapshots of the girls who'd been at the home a week ago, printed on plain white paper on the office ink-jet. Susanna had typed in information: the girls' names, ages, birth dates, where they'd come from, how they'd arrived at La Casa. She'd wanted more than the usual documentation. *Just in case,* she'd told him.

Cate went through every page, blue eyes studying each face, then returned to the top page and stared. Justin had taken the picture himself on a visit a few months ago. He'd already memorized all the details. Men were supposed to be the less sensitive sex, and Cate had always thought that applied double to him, but the moment he'd focused the camera, he'd known he was taking a picture of a man in love. Trent had never looked at Cate that way, not even when he was vowing to love and honor her forever.

Did it hurt her to see him looking at Susanna that way? Justin could identify worry, a little fear, a lot of affection, but nothing that suggested pain. Good. He didn't want her hurting for what she couldn't have.

He didn't want her hurting for another man.

With a sigh, she straightened the papers and put them back in the file before handing it to him. "They're so obviously in love. The way she's looking at him… I never looked at him that way. I never felt about him that way."

Something eased in Justin's chest. Damned if he

wanted to consider it closely enough to recognize it as relief, but it was, plain and simple.

She stood and filled her arms with stuff. "I'm going to get ready for bed. You need the bathroom first?"

He shook his head.

She was past him and halfway to the other room when she turned back. "When we're in Atlanta tomorrow…Trent's cousin, Rick, the GBI agent…that's where he's assigned." She raised one hand awkwardly when he started to protest. "Just think about it, will you?"

When the sound of the shower reached him moments later, along with the image of Cate, naked, wet, hair slicked back from her face, he surged to his feet, grabbed the room key and went outside. He'd spotted a convenience store across the street when they'd pulled in, and he headed that way.

The store was brightly lit, the gas pumps busy. He dodged a couple of cars and a half-dozen people to get inside the door and trolled the aisles, picking up everything that looked remotely snackable. Tomorrow he needed to do some real shopping—the only clean clothes he would have left was a pair of socks—or do laundry. If he'd realized when he'd packed that he was actually leaving the country, he would have done a better job of it.

He returned to the room with two grocery bags and a six-pack of bottled water. The other water, the shower, was quiet now—he'd never known a woman who could shower as quickly as Cate—and about the time he laid the bags on the dresser, the bathroom door opened. He looked into the mirror over the dresser, his gaze connecting with hers.

Damn, she was beautiful. Her hair *was* damp, slicked back from her face, and fragrances drifted on the steamy air escaping the bathroom. He would recognize the scent of her in his sleep: not just perfume, but lotion, face cream, shampoo, shower gel. The kind of sweet that stirred heat and need.

She stopped just outside the door, her gaze locked on his. Awareness flickered in her eyes. Wariness. Longing, though faint, as if she hadn't fully acknowledged it.

The air was heavy, charged. Warmth seeped through him, and when she moistened her lips with her tongue, his body turned hot enough to combust. Only a few feet separated them. He could cover it in two steps, take those clothes from her, give her something else to cling to and kiss her. Just one kiss. That would be more than enough for now...would never be enough.

He forced his gaze from hers, drew strength he didn't know he possessed and looked down, over pajamas covered with flamingos, fuzzy slippers and red toenails, then managed a sorry excuse for a smile. "Another niece?"

She nodded.

"I never thought of you as a pink person." His voice was husky, a parched sound from a throat too constricted to swallow.

So was hers. "You never thought of me as a person at all."

"Not true. I thought you were a beautiful pain in the ass who was interfering with my fun."

"I thought you were a handsome pain in the ass who was interfering with my marriage." Finally she took a step, but not toward him. To the bed, where she stuffed the ball of dirty clothing into the vinyl bag. "Deep inside, of course, I knew that wasn't true."

"The handsome part? Or the pain-in-the-ass part?"

She smiled tautly. "The interfering-in-my-marriage

part. If Trent had cared, no one could have made him behave the way he did."

Justin wrenched a bottle of water from the plastic liner and took a long drink. "He cared. He just—"

"—cared more about himself. He's not like that with Susanna. He would die—" Her face flushing, she broke off, and her hands trembled when she zipped the suitcase and heaved it to the floor.

Silently he offered her a bottle of water, which she accepted, and junk food, which she didn't. He swept his backpack to one side of his bed, folded back the covers and lay down, turning to face her. "They're okay, Cate."

There was too much hope, too much wanting to be convinced, in her eyes. He prayed he wasn't offering false hope, because he wanted to be convinced, too.

When she remained silent, he used the remote to switch on the television, then shut off the bedside lamp. It was too early for sleep, apparently for her, too, so they both settled in and he began flipping through the channels, finally stopping on a cooking show.

After a while, he went to the bathroom and turned off the light over there on his return. He switched off the only remaining light, right in front of the door, and by the flickering light of the TV, he eased back into bed, lowering the sound. "What made you decide to become a doctor?"

"My grandfather said I was born to be one. It's all I ever wanted. Well, for a while, when I worked for our vet after school, I considered being a vet. After all, dogs and cats don't argue with you."

"Yeah, but people don't generally bite."

She gave him a wry look. "You haven't spent enough time in the E.R. I've had plenty of biters, most of them adults. I've been bitten, spat on, punched and puked on and had things thrown at me that you don't want to know about."

"You don't get paid enough."

"Any doctor who's in it for the money needs his head examined. It's a tough job. You make a mistake, someone can die."

"Has that happened to you?"

"Not that I'm aware of, thank God."

The annoying music and loud voices of an infomercial came on the TV, and rather than change channels, Justin shut it off. Darkness settled over the room.

"What was the one thing you wanted most?" she asked after a bit.

Sitting up, he pulled off his clothes, tossing them to the floor, then slid under the sheet in his boxers. The only honest answer he could give was the one she already knew, and it embarrassed him. "To have fun. I never really wanted for anything. My parents spoiled me. They gave me everything, including their attention. Neither they nor my grandparents have ever had actual jobs. They do charitable stuff—organizing, fundraising, donating—and between that and their social obligations, they stay busy enough that they actually have staff to help out, but as far as a regular job…" Even though she couldn't see, he shook his head.

"Some people do. Some people give. They're all vital." She paused for a delicate yawn. "So you were happy being young and irresponsible until you nearly died in that accident. Then you realized you needed more."

"Yeah." He waited. "What? No smug remark about it taking a life-changing event to make me do what everyone else had already done and grow up?"

"No, not from me. I've seen people undergo life-changing events without changing one bit. They never appreciate what they have, what they've done, what they can do. I'm impressed."

Justin was practically speechless. Twice in one evening, she'd said that. Was saying it as strange to her as it was for him to hear it?

"This is weird," he said at last, determined to lighten the mood. "I've never laid in bed in the dark talking with a woman who wasn't in that bed with me. Wanna come over here and snuggle while we continue this conversation?"

"Is that what they're calling it these days?"

"You're not suggesting we might do something other than talk?" he asked innocently, focusing on the deeper shadow on the other bed that was her.

"Are you suggesting we wouldn't?"

He laughed. "It's nice to know I'm not the only one thinking that way."

Her voice sounded huffy, or maybe just muffled by the covers as she turned over. "As long as thinking is all we do…"

And now he wasn't going to be able to think about anything else.

His smile faded, and for a long time he listened to the sound of her breathing, slowing, steadying, lulling. When he was pretty sure she was asleep, he whispered, "Good night, Cate."

And after another long time, she whispered back, "Good night, Justin."

Thanks to Justin's heavy foot and a relative absence of troopers on the interstate, they reached their first destination in Atlanta just before eleven. They drove past the house belonging to Martin and Denise LeFrancois twice before he parked a few doors down on the quiet street.

"These two are both in internet businesses," Cate said while scanning Amy's email. "He's a partner in a search engine and online auction company, and her company provides virtual personal assistants to the rich and lazy. They share an office in the Peach Tree Complex. Their financial records do show payments to a pediatrician and a nanny—" a relieved sigh shivered through her "—but Amy didn't find any school records for seven-year-old Graciela."

She shifted her gaze from the tablet to the LeFrancois house. Like the Clarences', it was an old beauty kept in impeccable condition. Huge trees dominated the yard, a lot probably ten times the size of hers. A privacy fence of brick and wrought iron blocked the view into the back, and the four garage doors—*four,* with only two adults in the family—were all closed. "They're probably both at work. Doesn't anyone stay home these days?"

Justin gave her a wry look. "I don't know, *Dr.* Calloway. Would you give up medicine if a baby Calloway came along?"

"That isn't going to happen. I'm a doctor. I know what causes pregnancy and how to prevent it." Besides, though she hadn't told him, she agreed with his view. There were too many kids already in the world who needed parents. If she ever developed the longing for a child, she would adopt long before having one of her own.

"Hello."

His soft exclamation redirected her attention to the house, where the front door had opened and a young woman was maneuvering the Rolls Royce of strollers out onto the stoop.

"Come on, doc, let's go for a walk through our new neighborhood."

She got out hastily, stepping over a strip of grass lush enough for a country club to reach the sidewalk. Justin fell in beside her, taking her hand in his. Her fingers automatically curved to fit inside his, and once more that little sense of security quivered through her.

It was just a show, she reminded herself. They didn't want to arouse suspicion. Claiming to be husband and wife was one thing; acting the part was another.

The woman she presumed to be the nanny was nearing the end of the drive at the same time they approached. He smiled broadly and said, "Hey. Nice day, isn't it?"

Young, Latina, shy, the woman bobbed her head and would have gone on if Cate hadn't blocked her way. Crouching, she locked gazes with the blue-eyed, blond-haired baby strapped into the seat, probably about a year old, chubby-cheeked and fair, with two fingers in his mouth. He grinned without removing them.

"What a little sweetheart," Cate gushed—she, who had never gushed over a baby in her life, not any of her nieces, not even the first baby she'd delivered. "He's such a doll with those big blue eyes."

"Yes," the woman agreed with a nod and a move to leave.

Cate remained where she was, wrapping one hand around the padded bar at the front of the stroller as if she needed it for balance, and Justin launched into their cover story while she continued to coo at the little boy.

"My wife, Daisy, and I—"

She darted him a sour look, and he grinned expansively without missing a beat "—have just moved in down the street, and our neighbors said that a girl about the same age as our daughter, Lily, lives here. We'd love a chance for her to meet someone before she starts school next week. Are you Denise?"

The nanny's smile quavered as she shook her head emphatically. "Mrs. LeFrancois is at work. I take care of the baby." Her English was heavily accented, and her gaze darted everywhere except Justin's direction. "We must go now. Time for baby's walk."

Cate nearly lost her balance for real when the woman tugged on the stroller. She stood, smiling with as much forced warmth as she'd shown when she'd met Trent's parents for the first time. "It's a beautiful day for a walk. Do you take care of the LeFrancoises' little girl, too, when she's out of school?"

Darting a look over her shoulder toward the house, the nanny tightened her grip on the stroller and backed away a few steps. "There is no little girl. Just the baby. We must go."

"No little girl. Really, you're sure? Yeah, of course you would be. You live here, right?" Justin's smile was pleasant and charming but didn't reach his eyes. "I guess our neighbor must have been wrong. Have a good walk."

The woman swiveled the stroller in the opposite direction and walked along the sidewalk. Every few feet, she glanced back at them and picked up her pace a bit more until she and the baby were practically jogging. When they reached the corner two houses down, they turned and disappeared from sight.

"Who do you think she was scared of? Us? Mrs. Le-Francois?"

Justin, staring at the house, absently answered, "Or immigration. If the LeFrancoises went south of the border to get a kid, maybe they also got their nanny there.

How better to get good, cheap help than to hold arrest and deportation over their heads?"

After a moment, he took her hand. "Let's get out of here before someone who *is* home calls the cops on us for hanging around where we don't belong."

Still part of the show, she reminded herself. Nothing more.

It was a forty-minute drive across the city to the next house on their list. They stopped for lunch when they reached the area, then drove into yet another neighborhood of expensive homes. Unlike the last two, though, these houses were new, built to seriously impress, with tons of brick, slate roof tiles and columns on every other mini-mansion. Elaborate wrought-iron gates marked the entrance, but they stood open.

"No point living in a gated community if you're not going to close the gates," Justin murmured.

"Yours didn't do much to keep the Wallaces' punks out of your house," she reminded him drily.

"No, but these would have kept us out. I don't know how to bypass an electronic lock. Do you?"

"Sorry. They didn't teach that in medical school. There it is." She gestured to a faded brick monstrosity two blocks in on the left. The slate roof soared at so many angles it was dizzying to look at, and the leaded windows were tall and narrow, reminding her of defensive ports on centuries-old forts. The similarity summoned the far-from-reassuring thought of Mr. or Mrs. Grayson waiting behind one of those windows with a crossbow, a pot of flaming oil or an automatic weapon.

"You want to go or do you want me to?"

You go. Her stomach was knotted and her chest hurt as if she'd cracked a few ribs and couldn't breathe deeply. But when he parked a few feet in front of the garage, she undid her seat belt. "I'll go. I look way more harmless than you."

"I'm harmless," he protested, then grinned at her snort. "Go ahead, ring the bell. They're probably not home, either."

She was about to close the door when he leaned over. "I won't be able to see you at the door. Scream if you need me."

"I'm a great screamer." Hands clammy, she shut the door, then followed the curve of the sidewalk to double doors deep inside the entryway. The metalwork on the doors was iron, huge black straps that reminded her again of ancient fortresses. As a welcoming feature for the home, they fell far short of the mark. The bell echoed distantly, a discordant peal for attention. Not expecting an answer, she studied the iron sconces mounted on each wall, the worn brick beneath her feet and the sculpture to one side that was all sharp edges and angles. It looked as if it belonged in a torture chamber, not in the entry of a multimillion-dollar Atlanta home.

The door opening startled her, and she snapped a smile into place as she turned. Halfway through the motion, she lost the smile and the only turning she wanted to do also involved running. Her feet seemed frozen, though.

The man who stood in front of her—Hector Grayson, her brain supplied, though its fight-or-flight mechanism had apparently stopped working—was tall, muscle-bound and fierce. With salt-and-pepper hair pulled into a ponytail, heavy brows drawn together, a hawkish nose and a bandito mustache, under the best of circumstances he would have made her uncomfortable. Under *these* circumstances, she was having trouble breathing.

"It's for you," he said, his voice somewhere between

a growl and a snarl. When he thrust out his hand, she cringed, but still her body didn't heed her desire to flee. It took a moment to realize he held a phone in those thick fingers, a moment more to realize he expected her to take it.

Don't shake. Don't let him see he scared you. Aw, hell, it was way too late for that. She took the phone without touching him, barely managing to close trembling fingers around it, and lifted it to her ear. "H-hello?"

Grayson folded his arms over his chest and leaned against the jamb, watching, waiting, still scary.

"Dr. Calloway. I'd like to say it's a pleasure, but I'm sure you'll understand why I can't." The voice was male, lightly accented, smarmy and oozing with feigned graciousness. "I was under the impression that you and Mr. Seavers were looking for the records he helped steal from my employers."

"We—we are."

"And you believe they might be at Mr. Grayson's home? Or Mrs. LeFrancois's or Mrs. Clarence's?"

She didn't know what to say. Didn't have a clue. If she were braver, or more foolish, she would reply that he'd been under the impression that she and Justin were still in Cozumel; obviously, he was wrong. She would tell him that of course the records weren't at those people's homes, but then, neither were the girls they had supposedly adopted.

But she wasn't brave, or foolish, and she couldn't find the clearness of mind to form any response at all.

"I'm very disappointed, Doctor. I wonder why you and Mr. Seavers are harassing the foundation's clients. I wonder why you're not devoting your time to recovering the records, as we asked. I wonder why I should wait another hour to prove to you that this business is serious. I wonder why I'm not giving the order to dispose of Mr. Calloway as we speak."

"You don't want to do that," she blurted. Grayson's bored, disinterested manner made her skin crawl, and she wanted to turn her back to him but couldn't do it. Instead, she took a few steps to the side so the brick wall of the entry was behind her and he was in her peripheral vision. "You want the files back, don't you?"

"I'm not so sure now. You've apparently found someone who can decrypt them."

"Only one. Only the file with the girls' names and the parents they were placed with. That's it. Nothing else. And we can recover the flash drive with the rest of the files. We just need a little more time."

"Where are they?"

"We're not sure yet. Justin and Susanna overreacted. They wanted to get the flash drive with the files as far away from them as possible, in a place where you could never find it. They passed it off to a friend who gave it to another friend who gave it… You get the idea."

The man chuckled. "Amateurs. They should never have taken it from the island."

"They should never have taken it from the foundation," she pointed out, and he laughed again.

"I like you, Dr. Calloway. You're pragmatic. If you ever decide you want to live in paradise, we could find a place for you at the foundation." When he spoke again, the good humor was gone from his voice. "Leave our clients alone. Get the files. We'll give you forty-eight hours to contact us. Mr. Grayson will give you the number. After that, start checking the news reports for Cozumel. You never know when another body will wash up onshore. Unfortunate boaters, fishermen…divers. Good day, Doctor."

The call clicked to an end. Dazed, she listened to silence for a moment before Grayson's movement made her stiffen. He held out one hand for the phone, a slip of paper in the other. When they'd made the exchange, he growled, "Get off my property before I throw you off. And if you come back, I'll drag your scrawny ass inside and shoot you for an intruder. Got that?"

Eyes wide, she started to nod, then decided to hell with it. Spinning, she rushed back to the car, fumbled with the door, with getting in, with the seat belt, chanting as soon as she got in, "Let's go, let's go, let's go."

Thankfully, Justin didn't ask questions; he shifted into Reverse, backed out fast and headed toward the gated entrance at a fair rate of speed. Once outside the gates, Cate eased her grip on the door handle a bit; after they'd put several more blocks between them and Grayson's subdivision, her heart slowed enough that cardiac arrest didn't seem imminent.

She was in the middle of her first deep breath in a long time when Justin abruptly cut in front of an oncoming car and turned into a strip-center parking lot. Her head whipped around, searching for something suspicious behind them, but she saw nothing. Just life as usual on an Atlanta afternoon.

Would she ever have a *life as usual* again?

Instead of finding a parking space, he drove behind the shops, about halfway down the length of the building, where a row of Dumpsters blocked them from the street. He shut off the engine, got out and came around to her side of the car. His hands were unsteady as he loosened the seat belt, then he lifted her out of the car, pulled her close and wrapped his arms tightly around her.

He felt so solid and strong, and she'd been scared forever, it seemed. Her knees gave way, and she sagged against him, face pressed into his shirt, shudders rico-cheting through her. She'd been threatened before, but by patients who talked a lot and were rarely in a condition to act. But this man on the phone, and Grayson—they could both act and feel no remorse. Grayson could have snapped her like a twig before she'd been able to do more than croak Justin's name.

He stroked her hair, but this time he didn't bother assuring her that everything would be okay. They were long past the *okay* mark, and she didn't know if they would ever find it again.

Slowly the rush of emotion that made her feel so fragile passed, but she didn't step away. Instead, she wrapped her arms around him, clasping her hands behind him, standing as close as she could. She was afraid in a deeply fundamental way she'd never known before, and he was the only safety she knew.

Her shivers had stopped and the pressure around her lungs lessened before she spoke. "When Mr. Grayson opened the door, he handed his phone to me. It was the man who's called you." Drawing comfort from him, she repeated the conversation, amazed by how many details her brain had stored in total recall in the midst of total panic.

"So either Mrs. Clarence or the nanny doesn't like uninvited guests."

"The nanny was scared. She probably called her boss as soon as she got away from us." Swallowing hard, she tilted her head to see his face. "He gave us forty-eight hours, Justin. If we don't call to arrange a time to return the files by then, they're going to kill Trent."

"Where's the number?"

For a moment she stared blankly, then let go of him. The paper was still crumpled in her left hand, the ink, thankfully, unsmeared. He tucked it into his pocket, then gazed into her eyes. "You okay?"

She nodded. It was a lie, and she was pretty sure he knew it. "We can't let them kill Trent."

"We can't," he agreed.

"But if we give them the files, they'll kill all of us."

"They will. I don't know about you, doc, but I'm not eager for that to happen." He pulled her to a nearby bench, used by shopping center employees on smoke breaks, judging by the number of cigarette butts on the ground around it. "You still think we should contact Trent's GBI agent cousin?"

The part of her that had just been threatened and insulted at the same time—scrawny ass, indeed—by a big scary guy wanted to say *hell, yes*. Some stronger part stopped her. "We have a deadline and not much to tell him. No proof that Trent and Susanna have actually been kidnapped. No proof that the Wallace brothers are involved. No proof that the girls were ever delivered to the parents on that list. No proof that the other encrypted files on the flash drive have any incriminating evidence in them. If we went to Rick, he would at least look into it, but it would take him more than forty-eight hours to learn anything. And if the Wallaces found out…"

"It would be too late for Trent and Susanna."

She scooted closer to him, until the warmth from his body seeped into hers. "And for us," she whispered.

He settled his arm over her shoulders as if it were the most natural thing in the world. "We need to find just one of those girls."

"How? If the Wallaces warned Grayson about us, they've probably warned everyone."

They sat in silence for a time. The air was warm, the street sounds muted. A plain board fence faced them on the opposite side, defaced—or maybe improved—by graffiti, and the odors from the Dumpsters mixed with leftover cigarette residue for an unpleasant perfume. It could have been worse, though. Apparently none of the Dumpsters were used by restaurants.

Looked like that might be her new motto: *it could be worse.*

"Okay," Justin said. "They know we're in Georgia, so let's have Garcia dig up what she can on the families out west. We can be on a plane headed that way in no time."

"But if the parents have been warned…"

"The logical thing for us is to go for the best access. Sixteen of those families live in the South, so we came here. The other six might think distance will protect them. That we'll continue to hang around where most of the kids are supposed to be. They might not take it as seriously as the ones here will."

"As seriously as Grayson *did,*" she added with a shiver.

"If we catch the Wallaces, we'll catch Grayson, too." He hugged her tight for a moment, then let go and stood, handing her the burn phone, keeping his own. "You call Garcia, and I'll see about the plane." Scrolling through phone numbers, he walked away from the bench, then turned back to grin at her. "He's wrong, you know. Your ass isn't scrawny at all. In fact, it's just about perfect."

Nothing could have made her laugh at the moment, unless it was the kind of laugh that led to hysteria. She would have thought nothing could have made her smile, either, but Justin's remark, along with that boyishly charming grin, did just that.

Chapter 8

One of the benefits to being rich was having rich friends. It took Justin ten minutes on the phone with an old friend from college to catch up on the last few years, ask after his family and arrange to borrow his private jet for a few days.

When he got off the phone, he listened to Cate's side of the conversation with Amy. "Which family?" Cate repeated. "How about the one least likely to threaten to shoot me?"

Amy's response made her brows lift. "You can do that? Wow, Amy, you really are the chief worker of miracles. We'll be checking for your email." Cate pressed the End button with one fingertip, then automatically handed the phone back. "She's going to check the remaining couples for arrest records."

"Does Grayson have one?" Of course Amy would have looked him up while they were talking.

"He's been arrested several times. He has anger issues."

Justin's stomach knotted. He'd offered to go to the door himself. Why in hell had he given her a choice? Grayson wouldn't have killed her because the Wallaces didn't want her dead—yet—but he could have hurt her badly with one punch, one bulldog grip or shove. And *he'd* sat in the car like an idiot, unable to see or hear her, thinking she couldn't be facing anyone more dangerous than Monette Clarence, who wouldn't have risked her manicure with physical violence, or the frightened nanny who would have run screaming if either of them had said *boo!*

He'd helped get her into this mess. If he couldn't keep her safe while she was in it, what the hell good was he?

He leaned against the car. "Where do your sisters live?"

She blinked, puzzled by the change of subject. "Two of them are still in Macon, one's in Charlotte and one's in Savannah."

"I can put you on a plane to Savannah. Better yet, do you have any friends that live out of state? Or what about that cop you used to date? Would he let you hide out with him for a while?"

She stood and closed the distance between them with long strides, her manner menacing despite the fact she was shorter, skinnier and so damn delicate looking. "No, you can't put me on a plane to Savannah. I'm not going to risk endangering my sister or her family. Yes, I have friends who live out of state, and yes, it would be harder for the Wallaces to connect me to them, but no, I'm not doing that, either. Yes, of course AJ would let me hide out with him, and even better, his wife, the woman he dumped me for, is an ex-homicide detective herself, but that's not happening, either. You're stuck with me, Justin. Just as we're stuck with the damn Wallaces."

When she stopped, she was standing so close. All he would have to do was shift his feet a few inches apart, slide his hands around her waist, nudge her an inch or two closer. It would be more intimate than they'd ever been, except for last night's talking in bed. Even though they hadn't even touched. Hadn't even been in the same bed.

"If anything happens to you…"

She came one step closer. "We'll have the Wallaces to blame."

"They wouldn't know you or Susanna existed if not for me."

"Don't kid yourself. Cozumel's not that big. They realized there was big money in abandoned kids, and Susanna was in the business of rescuing said kids. They would have found their way to her sooner or later."

It didn't ease the guilt nagging at him, but she was right. Joseph and Lucas Wallace were sharp businessmen, always looking for the next investment, the next big return on their money. Like sharks to chum, they would have found Susanna and La Casa on their own and been circling in no time.

Now they were going in for the kill.

"Did you get us on a flight?"

"I did. We have to be at the airport in an hour."

An hour, and the drive to the airport would take half of that. They'd already eaten lunch and managed to make it too dangerous to even drive past any of the other addresses in the metro area. Until they got word from Garcia, there was nothing else they needed to do.

There was no reason for him to push her back. No reason to rise from where he leaned, or to walk away from her, to get into the car with that safe distance of the center console between them. No reason to do anything but exactly what they were doing: standing so close that one deep breath would make their bodies touch, staring at each other like they'd never really seen each other before, waiting and wondering and wanting…

Of their own will, his hands settled at her waist. She was curvy for a woman shy of five and a half feet, with nice breasts, a slim waist and very nice hips that led to her amazing legs. The soft fabric of her clothes padded the toned body underneath, and warmth seeped into his hands while the mix of fragrances that would forever remind him of her scented the air.

"Would you ever have imagined ninety-six hours ago that you and I would be standing like this?" he asked quietly.

"Yes. But in my fantasy, I was clawing that smug smile off your face."

"No smugness, see?" He smiled to demonstrate.

She laughed. "You can't *not* be smug. It's a part of who you are. If a person gets to know you, they get used to it."

"You want to get to know me even better?" With his fingertips splayed on her spine, he brought her closer, just until they touched, just until he could feel heat and hunger and tension radiating from her body the same as his own.

She raised one hand to stroke his jaw, her fingertips skimming so lightly it was more a suggestion than a touch. It was tempting and tantalizing, and it took all his strength not to grab her hand and press it hard against his skin. "I'm tempted."

It was the sort of statement that was always followed by a *but*. "But?"

"Thirteen years and a couple days of hating each other, and now suddenly we're contemplating…"

"I contemplated it before." When her brows furrowed in a soft frown, he gave her a sly look. "I was young and stupid, and you were young and beautiful. Of course I contemplated it. But you were hooked up with Trent, and I didn't really like you, and you really didn't like me. But the thought still entered my mind."

Rolling her eyes, she smiled. "Of course it did. But you know what I'm saying. Thirteen years of knowing exactly where we stood with each other. No matter what else happened in life, I could count on you to be smug, arrogant and self-centered. And you know what they say about adrenaline, danger, near-death experiences."

He knew: heightened senses, increased vulnerability, reckless decisions. Who was to say they wouldn't wake up in a couple of days, when all this was hopefully and successfully over, look at each other and think, *Dear God, what have I done, and how do I get out of it?*

"I've experienced adrenaline rushes, dangerous situations and near-death experiences before, and they've never made me want to run out and commit to the first woman I laid eyes on."

She blinked that slow blink that made her look cuddly as a small bird. "Did you just say 'commit'?"

"I did." And he made no effort to recall it. "I'm thirty-four, Cate, and I've been a responsible adult for six years." He grinned at the implication of that statement. "I don't fool around like I used to. I actually have friendships and relationships with women now. I take all of them seriously. You can't commit to a lifetime together if you can't commit to a relationship to start."

She stared at him a long moment. "Wow, you've actually been listening to Susanna and all her psychosocial stuff, haven't you?" Then, without warning, she leaned forward, wrapped her arms around his neck and kissed him, hard and sweet and needy and enticing, a claiming, demanding, pushy sort of kiss that she ended too soon.

"Garbage truck is coming. We should go." She stepped away and went to the car door, but it was obvious that she wasn't nearly as unaffected as she pretended. Her voice was husky and her hand trembled as she opened the door. If it had taken her one second longer to slide inside, he would have bet her legs would have collapsed beneath her. When she assumed he couldn't see her, she touched shaking fingers to her lips for a moment, then clasped her hands in her lap.

Justin breathed deeply as the racket from the garbage truck at the far end of the alley echoed from fence to building. He tried willing his body systems to settle back to normal. His lungs and heart cooperated—grudgingly—and his temperature began cooling.

But it was going to be a while before this damn erection went away.

They pulled away from the Dumpsters ahead of the garbage truck, driving to the end of the alley, then turning into the parking lot. Cate expected Justin to head out onto the street, but instead he parked in front of a discount clothing store. Still a little shaken—and breathless—she glanced his way.

"I need clothes," he said in response.

She would have liked to wait in the car, except that she was too scared. Climbing out, she started across the lot with him, and she gave only the smallest of jumps when he took her hand.

Because this time it wasn't for show.

She'd never seen anyone shop as quickly as he did.

Trent was the only other man she'd shopped with, and while he preferred a casual, scruffy style, like Justin, it was a very carefully put together designer scruffy. Justin, on the other hand, located a display of shorts, picked up four pairs, then grabbed four T-shirts from a rack, two packages of boxers and a pack of socks. He didn't try anything on, wasn't fussy about colors or styles. In less than ten minutes, they were back in the car and on their way to the airport.

She wondered if the number had any significance. Like, if he didn't think they'd be alive long enough to need a fifth outfit. The possibility sent a shiver through her that she shook off as she dug a pair of nail clippers from her bag. "The variety of color in your wardrobe in amazing," she remarked as she began snipping tags from the shorts—all shades of tan.

"Sorry. I didn't think to pack my collection of vintage Hawaiian shirts."

"I bought AJ a Hawaiian shirt once. I think his new wife burned it."

"How could you get involved with a man who doesn't appreciate a good Hawaiian shirt? They're classic." He gave her a sidelong look, actually waiting for an answer.

"I wasn't aware of that when we started dating. That particular question was never on my checklist for potential mates." Her tone was dry, even as she thought back to her relationship with AJ. It had been great. They'd had a lot in common; the sex was always good; they'd just flowed naturally from friendship to dating to talking about marriage.

The end had come just as naturally. She'd emerged with her heart intact. She'd loved him—still did—but she hadn't been in love with him, nor he with her. They'd shared less passion in the year they'd been together than she and Justin had in the past few days.

That made her breath catch in her chest. She'd *loved* AJ. Was it even remotely possible that she could be falling in love with Justin?

Could she survive falling in love with Justin?

They'd reached the airport before she'd realized they had even left Grayson's neighborhood behind, but Justin bypassed the passenger terminals for a smaller, quieter building. "What airline are we flying?" she asked as he parked in a distant space.

"Westin Air." He waggled his brows as he cut the engine, then popped the trunk open.

The name sounded vaguely familiar, but she couldn't place it until she was rearranging the stuff in the duffel Justin had unzipped to make room for the new clothes. Alex Westin was a friend of Trent's, and therefore Justin's, from college—another trust-fund kid. They'd been in the same fraternity, traveled in the same social circles and shared the same taste for adrenaline. Alex had always been hanging out when she'd gone to the frat house to see Trent, and he'd come to the wedding, too. The biggest difference between him and Justin was that he'd never tried to warn her off Trent.

And he'd never been anywhere near as sexy as Justin.

"Alex has an airline?" She neatly folded two pairs of shorts and wedged them into the bag before Justin took the sackful of clothes and crammed it inside. He packed as if he'd learned in a sardine cannery.

"Better. He has a Gulfstream." He gestured to the tarmac behind the building, where a jet waited. Compared to the commercial plane that had taken her to and from Cozumel, this one was tiny, sleek and graceful in appearance, built for speed—and luxury, she saw, when the pilots met them inside and escorted them on board a few minutes later.

Wow. The cabin *smelled* like money, an intoxicating mix of buttery leather and exotic woods and plush carpet. In addition to a full couch, there were another half-dozen seats big enough to curl up in, a large-screen television and an array of electronics—stereo, DVD player, computer, fax, printer.

"Wow." This time she said it aloud. She put her bag on the couch before facing Justin. "This is amazing. Why don't you have one?"

"Why buy when I can borrow someone else's?" He settled into a chair and fastened his seatbelt. "For the record, everything in here is as green as it could be. Alex is big on environmental issues."

She slid into the chair across the table from him and buckled up, then rested her hands on the surface. That made three spoiled rich kids she knew now who were passionate about making life better for others. She really needed to adjust her attitude.

"Besides," Justin went on, "do you have any idea how many dive trips for the kids $35 million would cover?"

Her jaw dropped. She'd learned with the Calloways to disguise her awe most of the time. It wasn't as if she were poor. Her family had been solidly middle-class, with five daughters to raise, clothe and put through college. The Proctors had had enough for necessities, comfort and some luxuries, but a $35 million plane… "How much food and medicine," she murmured.

"Clean water. Shelters. Doctors." Justin's expression was part grimace. "To be fair, Alex uses the plane for more than dive trips or dinner in Paris with his latest girlfriend. He provides free transportation to medical volunteers in Central and South America. He brings kids who need extensive care to the U.S. with their families and pays their expenses while they're here. He makes the jet available to people on transplant lists who have to get to the transplant center on short notice, and he flies World War II veterans to visit the memorial in D.C."

Cate gazed out the window at the activity across the tarmac. She doubted any of her family or friends did that much with their favorite charities. Of course, their efforts would be on a much smaller scale, but they didn't even manage that. They wrote a check now and then or did hands-on volunteering from time to time, but she couldn't think of one who was truly passionate about it.

Her own involvement was much less substantial.

As if reading her mind, he said, "Hey, you do what you can. People have jobs, responsibilities, families. Alex doesn't have a job or any responsibility beyond spending the money he inherited."

She was beginning to see that could be a much bigger responsibility than she'd ever wanted to acknowledge.

"Can the Wallaces track us to Arizona?" she asked as the engines revved, restless for a change of subject. What did it say about her that she'd rather think about the people holding Trent and Susanna hostage than her preconceived—and wrong—notions?

"I don't know how. The pilots will file a flight plan, but they don't have to report that they're carrying passengers. The only people who know we're here are Alex and the pilots, and trust me—" his tone turned wry "—the pilots are well paid not to gossip."

As he finished speaking, the intercom hummed to life with the captain announcing they would be starting to taxi out. Justin was relaxed, sprawled in his chair, head tilted to one side and gaze fixed outside the window at the scenery slowly passing. His hair was mussed, his attitude one of ease. His features were so familiar, and yet different.

The difference, of course, wasn't in his face, but her. Instead of being the enemy, now he was a partner. A companion. Even—she'd never dreamed she might think this—a friend.

And the object of her latest fantasies. She had *kissed* him, for God's sake. She, who had never wanted to breathe the same air he breathed, had kissed him.

She could give several reasons for it that sounded credible enough. She'd been frightened. Her emotional control had been running thin. She'd wanted the power of a touch. It was human nature, wasn't it, to want physical contact in stressful moments. But the simple truth was, she'd wanted to. Wanted to be that close. Wanted to feel that intimate. To taste him, touch him, lean on him.

She'd *wanted*. Him.

The thought sent blood rushing to her cheeks and formed a knot in her stomach.

"What are you thinking to make you blush like that?"

His voice, throaty and amused, drew her attention back to the face she'd been staring at, and the heat in her own face climbed a little more. "N-nothing."

Then came the smug, cocky grin that used to make her want to smack him. "Were you imagining me naked?" He raised his hands in a helpless shrug, when he was anything but. "Women usually do. Better yet, were you imagining *us* naked? Because I have been, and that sofa makes into a damn comfortable bed." He watched her gaze flicker to the cockpit. "The pilots never come any farther back than the galley."

Slowly she shook her head. "I don't think so." It was eye-opening just how tempted she was, even though there were a thousand reasons why she shouldn't have been. It was risky. What if the Justin she loved to hate came back? What if this thing *was* just the side effect of adrenaline and fear? She didn't treat sex lightly. She wasn't a prude about it, but she'd never slept with a man she hadn't thought had the potential for a long-term place in her life. What kind of potential was there between her and Justin?

Besides great sex.

He lived in Mobile; her life was in Copper Lake.

He was filthy rich—generously rich, she corrected herself; her income wasn't shabby, but it didn't put her in his universe. Besides, she'd visited there while she was married to Trent and wouldn't fit in any better now than she had then.

He spent half his time elsewhere, taking chances, having fun, doing good; she liked staying at home, having a regular job, taking care of her little house and spending time with her friends who also had regular jobs and regular lives. She didn't take chances, and her idea of fun was tame and boring compared to his. Hadn't he reminded her just a few days ago that she'd bored Trent to tears?

And the biggest question: Was she willing to risk having her heart broken again?

Because no matter how readily she admitted Justin had changed, she just couldn't quite picture him in a happily-ever-after, especially with her. She couldn't quite *trust*.

And the thing was, she didn't know if it was him she couldn't trust...or herself.

Justin hadn't expected an affirmative response to his suggestion that they put the sofa to good use, but it would have been nice if she had at least agreed to pick up where they'd left off at the Dumpsters. That kiss had been sweet, and it had made him restless, wanting more, but there hadn't been any doubt to her refusal. Oh, maybe to her words—*I don't think so,* way better than *not in a million years*—but the shake of her head had been firm. He wasn't getting lucky on this flight.

Did she still distrust him? The idea nagged at him. Granted, as she'd said, they'd had thirteen years of knowing where they stood with each other, only to have things do a one-eighty now. He'd admitted to having been a jerk. He'd shown her—hadn't he?—that he'd grown up. And she'd kissed him. *She* had kissed *him.*

Maybe she was right. Thirteen years versus a couple of days…

But for a lot of those thirteen years, he'd been more of a person than she'd given him credit for. What would he have to do to get her to give that credit and a little bit more?

A whole lot more, he acknowledged. He wasn't even sure of exactly how much *more* he wanted. Sex, sure. Time together, right. A chance—a real chance—at whatever she might give. Whatever she *could* give. Maybe…

Forever.

Itching to move, he glanced out the window at the billowy clouds stretching endlessly beneath them, then released his seat belt and stood. "You want something from the galley? Water, pop, booze, chocolate?"

She shook her head, and he moved down the aisle to the forward galley. Of course it was well stocked; people who could afford private jets cared about that sort of thing. He debated over the choices before picking out a bottle of water and a banana.

Forever.

He'd always figured there would eventually be someone he'd think that way about. In his family, divorces were rare. Marriages lasted, though he wasn't sure that in some cases, it didn't have more to do with the fortunes involved than with love. But Seaverses took marriage seriously. That was one reason he'd never given it a lot of thought. Once he was in it, he was likely in it for good.

Well, that, plus the fact that he'd never met the woman he could face spending the next fifty years with. But if he considered it, if he mostly closed his eyes and squinted a little, he could see himself spending more time with Cate. Not days, not even months, but years, maybe. Forever. Maybe.

As he turned back toward the cabin, he kept his eyes wide open.

He bypassed the table where she sat and approached the aft workstation, booting up the computer, then settling comfortably into the chair. In less than five minutes, he had a video linkup with Garcia, sitting in front of the array of computers that filled one of her two offices. Her hair was straight today, as conservative in style as his mother's, though he doubted Mom would ever consider striping her blond hair with orange. The stud in Garcia's nose was small, discreet—a skull, he thought, though it was hard to be sure.

"Hello, my pretty," she greeted him. "Wherefore art thou?"

"Somewhere in the skies between Atlanta and Phoenix. You have anything for us?"

"I see you're traveling in style. You have a printer there?"

"I do."

With a flourish, she clicked the mouse a few times, then said, "Everything you could ever want to know about the non-Southern families on the list is coming your way. You can peruse it at your leisure." She smiled tightly, then asked, "How's Cate?"

He was about to answer when Cate slid into a chair beside him. All those scents of hers drifted on the air, so much richer than the expensive-jet smells. "I'm fine. Fully recovered from my encounter with Mr. Grayson."

"Huh. You're tougher than me, sweet pea. I'd still be peeking out from behind Justin."

"I wasn't much good at the time," he said drily. "I didn't even know…" But not again. Cate wasn't approaching anyone else by herself.

"Don't blame yourself, doll. Nobody's fault but the bad guys'. On the other files, I'm still hitting a brick wall, but if you hit it enough times, even the strongest wall will give eventually." Garcia's gaze flickered away from the camera. Her mouth thinned and the tightness in her expression increased when she looked back. "There, uh, is something else. I've been keeping an eye on the international news services and, uh…"

Justin's gut knotted. He didn't want to hear bad news. A jerk of his arm blamed on nonexistent turbulence, a click of the mouse, and the connection would be cut. But that would just be a temporary reprieve.

"What is it?" Cate sounded calm, though he could feel tension radiating from her, shimmering the air between them.

With a deep breath, Garcia rushed it out. "A man's body was found in Cozumel just an hour or two ago. No ID, nothing. He was apparently not a local, and he'd been beaten to death. They're waiting on a positive identification from fingerprints, but his description—height, weight, hair color, eyes—matches…" She faltered.

Trent.

"It's not him," Justin said flatly.

"I pray it's not."

"They gave us forty-eight hours." Yeah, they were killers, perverts and God knew what else, but they'd set a deadline. Surely they realized the deadline would mean nothing if they'd already killed Trent.

Except they would still have Susanna.

"We'll think positive thoughts," Garcia said, her voice forced into optimism. "We'll give them credit for being smarter and better and more honorable than they are. And I'll let you know ASAP if I find out anything new."

"Thank you, Amy," Cate said when he couldn't find any words.

The face that usually never failed to cheer him disappeared from the screen and silence settled over the cabin. He stared at the bulkhead, doing his damned best not to let images form in his brain. The body washed ashore on the beach. The last time he'd seen Trent. The first time he'd seen him. God, they'd been buddies half their lives after meeting on a dive trip when they were sixteen. He couldn't imagine… He *wouldn't* imagine.

Cate's hand on his arm startled him, his gaze jerking to her. She looked as serious as he'd ever seen her, as fearful. "He asked why he should wait another hour, why he shouldn't dispose of Trent now."

"He didn't do it."

"He could have. He'd still have leverage. He'd still have Susanna."

Justin scowled at her because deep inside he wanted to give in to the same fear. "It's not him. Why kill one of your hostages—the rich one, the one closest to the people you're trying to trade with?"

To prove to you that this business is serious.

That was what the bastard had told her, but she didn't repeat it now. She didn't need to.

Pressing his lips together, Justin shook his head stubbornly before meeting her gaze. "He's my best friend. It's not him."

If she noticed that his voice broke on the denial this time, she didn't show it except for the faint grip of her fingers on his arm before she let go and gestured to the computer. "Check your email. We need to have a plan when we get to Phoenix."

The gentleness in her words was almost his undoing. His hand trembled before he got a good grasp on the mouse, and his movements were jerky. When he signed in, a half-dozen files popped up, one for each of the families.

Once the printer started spitting out pages, he shoved the chair back and paced the length of the cabin. This wasn't the time to think about anything except Phoenix and what they would do there. It wasn't the time to feel at all. Trent was alive. Susanna was alive. And God help them, they were going to stay that way. So were he and Cate.

And Joseph and Lucas Wallace and that oily bastard who worked for them were going to die.

Or wish they had.

While the printer was running, Cate found clips in the desk drawer and separated the pages into families. The one in Phoenix had been the first file, so it was the first done. She scanned the pages, then went back to the first and read through. She was calm. *Tougher than me,* Garcia had said. Tougher than him, too. But then, she dealt with life-or-death situations on a regular basis. Being a good E.R. doc—and he'd never doubted she was a great one—required staying calm in crisis. She might melt down later, but right now she was in control.

"Their name is Sutton," she said, her attention still

on the pages, "and they live outside Chandler, Arizona, where they have a half-dozen thoroughbreds, a small kennel of registered champion German shepherds and—supposedly—one child. Luisa. The girl Susanna's volunteer friend tried to adopt."

The girl whose adoption had spurred all the questions and doubts.

"Neither Sutton has ever been arrested. She travels a good deal with the animals—she's going to a show in Los Angeles this weekend—and he…" Her nose wrinkled and loathing filled her voice. "He's a pediatrician."

First, do no harm.

The knot in Justin's gut worked itself a little tighter. "Anything suggesting Luisa is there?"

She flipped through the pages again. "No school records, no obvious child-related expenses, certainly no medical expenses. She's not on their medical or dental insurance, and she's not a beneficiary on their life insurance policies. No mention of her on Mrs. Sutton's blogs, no picture of her among the hundreds of shots of pampered pooches and horses."

A ghostly smile crossed her face as she held up the final page. "Amy included a satellite photo of the property. Oh, and the only expenses for an alarm system cover the barns and kennels, not the house. At least this time, we're not going in cold."

"This time you're not going in at all."

Her mouth flattened, her gaze narrowing. "Now, listen up, Justin—"

"No. We're partners in this mess, doc, but so far, you've approached all three families—"

"You were there with the nanny."

"—so now it's my turn."

Now she wore the scowl. It felt normal to have her

looking at him as if he were the most annoying thing in her world. Then the frown vanished and her expression softened, turned sympathetic and warm and concerned. "Okay," she agreed, laying her hand on his arm again.

And normal or not, that felt like the most *right* thing in his world.

Chapter 9

Amy had included more than the one satellite photo in the packet. One showed the house, no more than a hundred feet off the county road; another included the kennel and barn; the third extended beyond the edges of the property and gave a good view of the land across the road. It was unlevel, boulders jutting up here, rises sloping there. The nearest neighboring house appeared to be a half mile away, well out of sight of the Sutton home.

Cate had studied the pictures until the details were etched on her brain, through the rest of the flight, the drive to a hotel, the stop at a sporting goods store and, now, on the way to the Sutton house.

"The Suttons paid nearly double what the other family did," she remarked, as Justin exited the interstate in accordance with the GPS instructions. "Maybe the Wallaces realized they'd started at a lowball price and increased it to what the market would bear."

"Or maybe it was important to the pediatrician to have a kid under his control, so he wouldn't be tempted by his patients." A muscle twitched in his jaw, and his long fingers clenched the steering wheel.

"Or maybe he and his wife were already accustomed to paying outrageous sums for the animals they wanted." It would be a blessing if Luisa had been treated a fraction as well as those pricey horses and dogs, but the anxiety lodged in Cate's chest suggested that wasn't likely.

That ache had been there since the conversation with Amy. If the dead man was Trent…

No. She had to believe it wasn't. If the Wallaces had wanted to prove they were serious, Susanna would have made a more logical target. God love her—and Cate did—she was from a middle-class family in some small Idaho town, doing mission work in a foreign country. A lot of people would mourn her death, but it wouldn't come as a huge shock because sometimes mission workers died in foreign countries. It was a sad risk that came with the job, one that people accepted.

But Trent… His family was rich and powerful. They would create such a firestorm of bad press that both the American and Mexican governments would be forced to get involved. The Calloways would *never* just accept the murder of their son. They would demand justice.

It was just a coincidence—the timing, the physical similarity. If the Wallaces had wanted to send her and Justin a message, they would have used Susanna, and…

Relief washed over her. "It's not Trent. The dead man's not him." As he slowed for a stop sign, Justin looked at her, brow raised, and she couldn't help but smile, though her relief simmered with guilt. Whoever the dead man was, he was still someone's loved one. "They sent you that photo, remember?"

"How could I forget?"

"They sent you the picture to show you what they were capable of, to convince you to take them seriously. If they'd killed either Trent or Susanna to drive the point home, they would have let us know. There's no point in sending a message if they don't make sure we get it." Her voice trembled. "It's not Trent."

He held her gaze a long time, then slowly the tension drained from his face. The fear left his eyes, and the muscle in his jaw stopped twitching. He didn't grin or pump his fist in the air or let out a huge whoosh of gratitude. He just stared at her, then turned his attention back to the road, making a right onto the Suttons' highway.

Though he faced away from her, she heard his whisper. "Thank God."

A mile or more passed before he spoke again. "Okay, so we're agreed on the plan. According to Garcia and the credit card activity, Mrs. Sutton and the horses she's showing are well on their way to L.A. We'll scope out the place tonight, then come back early in the morning, before the pervert doc leaves for work. And after he's gone, *I'll* check out the house while you wait in the car."

She'd agreed to that on the plane, mostly to keep him from blaming himself for her confrontation with Grayson, but she hadn't actually promised. She was surprised he'd thought she had. "We'll play it as it comes."

His narrowed gaze flickered to her, then back to the winding road. "You can wait in the passenger seat or the trunk. It's your choice."

She looked at the photo on top of the stack of papers, comparing the roads to the map on the GPS screen. Let him take her silence for agreement. Her real answer was clear enough to her, though: *we'll see.*

"The Sutton house should be around this next curve on the left."

Now his mouth thinned to match his glare. "Cate, I will tie you up in the trunk. I'm not letting you take that kind of risk again."

An unamused laugh burst from her. "You're not *letting* me? Are you kidding? You're not my father, my grandfather, my boss, my husband, my boyfriend or my conscience. You're not in any position to *let* me do anything."

The muscle twitched again in his jaw. "I'm not gonna put you at risk, Cate. I'm not gonna lose you."

For a moment, all she could think was *Wow*. That sounded serious, like when he'd used the *C* word the night before. On Monday she'd gone to Cozumel to treat a few patients and enjoy a visit with Trent and Susanna, and on Thursday here she was in Arizona with Justin Seavers talking about commitment and him losing her. She couldn't have imagined so different a situation if she'd tried.

And the scary thing was, she didn't *want* to imagine a different situation. Oh, sure, she'd much prefer that Trent, Susanna and the girls were safe and happy and healthy, but for her and Justin…

When only four days ago there had never been and didn't seem could possibly ever *be* a her and Justin.

White board fence appeared on the left, signaling the beginning of the Sutton property. It was exactly the sort of fence she would imagine keeping horses in their Kentucky pastures, but here it was an odd contrast to the desert landscape made up of mostly scrub, cactus and rock. It ran straight and true to the driveway, where pipe painted white led to the house and, beyond, the outbuildings.

Unlike the other houses they'd visited, this one, though large, wasn't particularly imposing, at least from the outside. It was simple in design, two stories, white, with a broad porch. The buildings that housed the animals were much larger, elaborately landscaped, much more impressive.

"The barn and kennels make the house look like an afterthought," Justin said as he slowed.

"I guess champion breeding stock get to live like kings." While orphaned little girls…

An oversize SUV was parked in the driveway beside steps leading to the porch, and lights shone in a few downstairs windows, uncurtained thanks to the lack of nearby neighbors. Was Luisa in there now, having dinner with her adoptive father? Was one of those dark upstairs windows her room, painted pink or lavender, filled with stuffed animals and dolls, or did it hold the toys a pedophile preferred? Did she go to bed each night saying a prayer for the wonderful life she now lived, or did she cry herself to sleep, wishing she were back at La Casa, safe and loved?

As the board fence came to an end, Cate checked the photo again. "Up here on the right, there's a cleared space where we can pull off the road."

Neither of them had specified what "scoping out the property" meant, but she had a fair idea from the purchases he'd made at the sporting goods store: a pair of jeans and lightweight jackets for each of them; a couple of powerful mini-flashlights; a pair of night-vision binoculars and two cans of pepper spray. It wasn't the same strength the police used, the salesman warned, but it was still good for self-protection.

How much protection would it afford against big ugly guns?

Justin turned into the clearing and stopped. It looked as if it had been scraped clean for a onetime construction site. Dozed trees and bushes were mounded to one side, and a heap of rotted boards were piled in the middle. Either would hide the car from passersby.

After surveying the area, he grinned at her. It was the first grin since they'd talked to Amy, and it sent warmth and reassurance through Cate's veins.

"I'm hungry. Are you?"

"You're always hungry. How come you don't weigh four hundred pounds?"

"Do you know how many calories you can burn in an hour underwater? Between 550 and a thousand. Downhill skiing? Six hundred. Mountain climbing? About seven hundred."

"Yeah, well, I don't do any of that stuff, and twelve-hour shifts in the E.R. don't burn as many calories as you'd think."

His smile came slowly, strengthening as his gaze moved from her face to her chest, over her waist and hips, and rested a moment too long on her legs. Self-consciously, she uncrossed, then recrossed them. "Let me teach you to dive. Or ski. Or mountain climb. Better yet, we can forget all that and make up our own workout. No equipment necessary but what God gave us."

He slid his palm so lightly over her hair that she might have imagined it, but there was nothing insubstantial about his fingertips on her neck, coaxing her toward him. If she leaned forward a few inches, and so did he, they would definitely be within kissing distance, and if he kissed her, she would kiss him back, no doubt about it. She knew in her head that caution was always a good thing, but her heart could throw caution to the wind as quickly as Justin could.

Maybe she was a bit of a risk taker after all.

She let him nudge her almost close enough, then she laid her hand on his chest and pushed back. Just a bit of a risk taker, remember.

"Okay, okay." Her voice was hoarse enough to embarrass her. "I'm hungry, too." Before the cocky grin could return, she hastily added, "For food."

The sun was setting when they found a restaurant ten miles away, turning the sky delicate pastel shades that faded into blue and purple before finally giving way to night.

By the time they finished off greasy burgers and the best onion rings she'd ever had, the sky beyond the reach of streetlights and civilization was velvety black, dotted with tiny pinpoints of stars. While he fiddled inside the car, Cate shrugged into the new jacket to cut the evening's chill, then stood there, staring upward, sending quiet pleas to anyone up above who might listen.

Let the girls be safe and unharmed. Let Trent and Susanna survive. Let Justin and me survive.

Don't let him break my heart.

The car's interior lights went dark, though both front doors stood open. Grinning, he slid out of the driver's seat, then retrieved the rest of their purchases from the trunk.

He offered her a flashlight, which she tucked into her left jacket pocket. Next he took out both pepper sprays, the cylinders seeming small in his large hand as he shook them the way the sales guy had instructed. "If I give you one of these, will you promise not to spray me with it?"

"Okay." She reached, but he caught her hand with his free hand.

"Huh-uh. Not enough. I've noticed you say 'Okay,'

when what you really mean is 'I plan to do what I want, but maybe I'll let you in on it first.' I want a promise. The kind you don't break."

She lifted her left hand as if in court. "I swear by my Hippocratic oath."

His face wrinkled into a frown. "Hm. Let's see... You've smacked me. Pinched me. Threatened to claw my face off. I'm not sure that oath is strong enough."

Lazily she took the steps necessary to bring her body in contact with his. Her mouth brushed his jaw before reaching his ear, where she murmured, "I swear if you don't give me that pepper spray, I *will* use it on you the first time you go to sleep and leave it unprotected." Wiggling her fingers into the fist where he clenched the two cans, she got a grip on one and worked it free.

He stopped her own victory smile by pressing his forehead to hers, staring into her eyes. "Sweetheart, I don't leave *anything* unprotected around you. Especially me."

The words stilled her in the act of stepping back. Her breath caught in her lungs, and the elephant tumbled a time or two in her stomach. She strained a little closer, until her nose bumped his, then murmured, "That might be the sweetest thing you've ever said to me." That he considered her a risk. That he was vulnerable to her.

Something swept through her—warm enough to flush her skin, cold enough to raise goose bumps. Something optimistic and pessimistic and full of potential, good and bad. Something hopeful.

As she'd done, he brushed his mouth across her jaw, leaving a fiery, tingling trail behind, then whispered into her ear, "If you're through promising things you aren't going to deliver, we'd better get going." He backed off, turned her to face the car and nudged her into the passenger seat.

Was he talking about her refusal to be pinned down on issues like staying out of the way or taking orders? Or getting close to him, touching him, kissing him, if she had no intention of following through?

She knew anatomy down to the tiniest, most insignificant bone, muscle and nerve, but she was learning something new: the heart had a will of its own. Her head might know all the reasons a relationship with Justin would be bad, but her heart only knew that she felt safe with him. Comfortable. Protected. Wanted. Her head could keep him at a distance, but her heart had developed a bit of a defiant streak. It might be willing to sacrifice her well-being for its desires.

And she might be willing to let it.

The ten miles back to the clearing passed much more quickly this time. There was no moon tonight, and once Justin shut off the headlights, darkness settled around them. All he heard in the sudden quiet was the pops and clicks of the engine settling and the beat of his own heart. He opened the door, glad the overhead light he'd disconnected didn't give away their presence, and picked up the binoculars from the console. He didn't even suggest that Cate wait in the car.

He pushed his door shut with a quiet thud, and she did the same, then met him at the front of the car. The jeans she'd picked fitted her nearly as well as the dive skin, hugging thighs and hips and butt before she tugged down the jacket to cover everything interesting.

"Is it too cold for snakes to be out?" she whispered.

"It is. Snakes like the heat."

"What about spiders and tarantulas and Gila monsters? Is it too cold for them?"

He didn't have a clue about the temperature preferences of desert residents but figured it was in her best interest to pretend he did. "Yeah. Everything's tucked away in its burrow or web or wherever the hell it lives until the sun warms things up tomorrow."

"Good. Then we go that way." She pointed to a boulder on the west side of the clearing. At first she led the way, then they walked side by side until they reached the scrub. She wasn't great at following, he'd noticed, but she didn't hesitate to slide in behind him when the going got rougher.

It would have been easier with a full moon. Dressed all in dark as they were, they wouldn't have stood out against the landscape. Instead, they used the flashlights, sheltering them in their hands to minimize detection until they reached a vantage point directly across from the Sutton house.

He did a quick scan of the ground with the light before dropping down behind the cover of a low, sloping boulder. He wasn't any more anxious than she to make the acquaintance of Arizona's creepier life forms, not that he'd admit it.

The only exterior lights across the road, besides a lone pole lamp that shone on the SUV, were back by the kennels and barns. Those were lit up as if it were midday, making the shadows around the house seem deeper, starker. Lights were on upstairs now, muted by curtains but seeping out from two front windows, two side windows. Weaker light came from downstairs—the kitchen, he saw when he focused the binoculars. It was at the back of the house, on the other side of a large, unoccupied living room. The distortion made him squint and turned his stomach queasy, but what he could see of the room was functional but dated. Neither Sutton was much of a cook or surely they would have modernized the appliances and countertops in the past forty years.

As he panned across the room, shock stabbed through him. "Luisa," he whispered, jerking to a stop on the slight form standing at the kitchen sink. She wore a shapeless dress, was barefooted, and her ragged haircut looked as if it had been self-inflicted.

Cate, on her belly beside him, was damn near vibrating with the need to see for herself, her hands half-extended, her fingers shaking. He handed the binoculars to her, and she zoomed in on the large picture window that showed through to the kitchen. "Oh, my God, it *is* her."

"How does she look?"

"Green" was her immediate response. "Thinner than in the photograph. Someone did a whack job on her hair. She's scrubbing the sink like an expert. Do you suppose that's what they wanted her for—a servant?"

"When you buy someone, I think that makes her a slave." Then he shoved his fingers through his hair. "Maybe she's just doing her chores. Most kids have chores, right?"

She took her gaze from the binoculars for a moment. "Aw, that's cute. The trust-fund baby knows what chores are. Did you have any?"

"I went fishing with my grandfather every Saturday six months of every year until I turned sixteen."

"Fishing's not a chore."

"Doing it with my grandfather was."

She focused on the scene inside the house again. "My sisters and I set the dinner table, cleared it, did the dishes, made our beds, cleaned our rooms, helped with the yard work, did our own laundry by the time we were ten and ran most of the errands once we got our drivers' licenses." A sigh escaped her. "Maybe she is just doing chores, but she seems…withdrawn. Sad."

"Missing her mom?"

"Missing La Casa?"

Or maybe dreading bedtime? God, Justin couldn't even bear to think of it.

He rolled onto his side, watching Cate and the sky. She continued to study the Sutton house and the property, and the sky did nothing besides give way to the occasional streak of a shooting star. Did Luisa see the stars? Did she know the American custom of wishing on one?

He did. He made a lot of wishes on the first one, beginning with Luisa, Trent and Susanna, and ending with Cate.

Propping his head on one fist, he watched her. "Tell me, doc, do you always overthink your relationships?"

If the subject change surprised her, she didn't show it. "Only the important ones."

"You didn't overthink it with Trent."

"No," she agreed. "I didn't think that one through enough."

"How about the one with the cop?"

"AJ? We were friends, we dated, we had sex, we talked about marriage. It just sort of happened."

"So what you're saying is the only one you're over-thinking is me. Which makes me an important one."

That brought her attention back from the house. "No, that's not…but…"

It clearly frustrated her that she couldn't argue with her own words, and that made him grin. "The ones you don't think much about don't last. So you're thinking too much about this because it *could* last." His vision now accustomed to the dark, he recognized the somberness of her expression, though he had to strain to hear her words.

"Because it could end badly."

He was glad she could acknowledge that. "You could break my heart."

She snorted.

"What? You don't think I have a heart to break?"

"I think I could stop it, restart it and change its rhythm, and with time, medication and compliance, I could heal it, but break it? Me? I don't think so."

He touched her hair, sleek silky strands tucked behind her ears, and she went still, her breath little more than a whisper in the night. "You don't give yourself enough credit, doc."

For a long moment she continued to watch the house—more because she didn't want to look at him, he thought, than because she did want to look at Luisa. Finally, though, she glanced his way. "Our lives are very different."

"Are they? I go to bed at night. Do you? I get up in the morning and eat breakfast. I bet you do, too. I take care of what's on my schedule, I pay my bills, I visit my family, I hang out with friends. I clean my house, I wash my dishes, I do my laundry and I spend time giving a little help where it's needed. Which of those things do you not do?"

She blinked. "You clean your house?"

"Yeah. I know, you assumed I have a housekeeper. I don't. But I do admit to having a lawn service take care of the yard both in Mobile and Coz since I do travel a lot."

"I hardly travel at all. And certainly not in first class or by private jet when I do."

"Is travel a deal breaker? You can't fa—" he bit off the word and substituted another "—get involved with someone who travels? Even if everything else is good? Even if you're happy and having a great time and the sex is incredible?"

"Don't be ridiculous. And what makes you sure the sex would be incredible?"

He gave an exaggerated eye roll. "Because we're talking about me, right?" Then his voice got husky. "And you. You're special, Cate. Don't try to kid yourself you're not. And this thing between us… It's special, too. You know it is, or you wouldn't be afraid."

It was probably an effect of the night, but in that moment she looked softer, more vulnerable, more desirable than he'd ever seen her. She opened her mouth, then closed it, and closed her eyes, too, as if seeking another argument or the courage to give in to his.

Another argument won. "You live in Mobile. My life is in Copper Lake. I've been there a long time. I love my job and my friends and my home."

"There are airplanes, trains, buses and cars running both ways." He was silent, considering the wisdom of what he was about to say, then said it anyway. "I'm not tied to Mobile, Cate. I mean, I've lived there all my life except for college, and my parents are there, and I'd hate to leave the kids at the center, but nothing says I *have* to live there. I've just never found a good enough reason to move."

She stared at him a long time, making him wish he could see her eyes, see what thoughts were going through her head. That they were getting way ahead of themselves, probably. That agreeing to see each other was a long way from making a life together. That the future they were discussing might never come. That a relationship between them could dwindle off into nothing, just like other relationships in their pasts.

But then, she was the expert at overthinking. He knew what he wanted, and if she wanted him, too, they could find a way to make it work.

"Maybe you give me too much credit," she murmured before raising the binoculars again.

She didn't believe she could break his heart. Didn't believe he could want her, need her, love her enough.

He stared into the sky again, frustrated with her, with himself, with Trent and the cop and every other man she'd been with. It took a few deep breaths to blow out the irritation, a few deeper ones to calm himself. In another thirty-six hours, this mess would be over, one way or another. If they were still alive, if their lives went back to normal and he was still coming around, still coaxing her, still showing that he wanted her... Sooner or later, she would have to give him a chance, wouldn't she?

With a sideways glance, he reminded himself who he was talking about: Cate Calloway, queen of hardheadedness.

But *he* was the king of stubborn. He could show her he was serious, not with words but with actions.

"Luisa's leaving the kitchen."

He rolled onto his stomach in time to see the kitchen go dark. No lights came on over the stairs. Either she was making her way up in the dark, or—

Dim light appeared from beneath the porch, filtered through curtains or shades. If the Suttons had bothered with landscaping around the house, it wouldn't have been visible, but there it was, three narrow rectangles.

"A basement. And I can't see a damn thing."

Cate handed the binoculars to him, and he took a look. Six windows along the foundation, no more than a few inches above the ground, small, screened. "Maybe doing laundry is part of her chores."

Then the lights went off in the center windows, and a moment later the third window turned dark, too. Except for what appeared to be the master bedroom, the house was pitch-black.

"Do you think she sleeps in the basement?" Cate's voice quavered. "She's eight years old living in a four-thousand-square-foot house with two adults, and she *sleeps* in the *basement?*"

"It could be worse, doc."

She could be sleeping upstairs with the perv while his wife was gone.

A hell of a lot worse.

"There are no guarantees in life." Staring at herself in the bathroom mirror, Cate softly repeated the response her grandfather had always given her and her sisters when they complained. *You work hard, you do your best, you take the chances the good Lord gives you.*

She'd worked hard and done her best at everything else, but not in her love life. Instead of trying to resolve issues with Trent, she'd grown resentful. Instead of holding out for real true love and happily ever after, she'd settled for good enough with AJ. Instead of taking chances, she'd wanted the sure thing.

On the surface, Justin was *not* a sure thing. But the surface was just that. Deep inside... He wanted her. He wasn't promising forever; it would be nice, but no one could do that with certainty. Life got in the way. People changed. Hearts broke. But he was offering the next best thing: an opportunity. A commitment. In the end, it could come to nothing, or it could be—*he* could be—the best thing that ever happened to her. He could break her heart, or he could be the one she was meant to spend the rest of her life with.

Wasn't one worth the risk of the other?

Steam fogged over the bit of mirror she'd cleared, making her image ghostly before obscuring it completely. She didn't need to see to comb her hair, to brush her teeth or to add her damp towels to the pile left from Justin's shower. She gathered her dirty clothes, opened the door to a blast of cold from the room and stepped out, leaving the light on, the door mostly closed.

He was lying on his stomach in bed, wearing nothing but boxers, studying a sheaf of the printouts Amy had sent. He glanced her way, then grinned. "Another niece?"

The pajama pants she wore were white with brightly colored owls, topped by a blue T-shirt embroidered with a trio of the birds. "We always have pajama parties when I visit. They take the pajama part of that very seriously."

"You remind me of an owl sometimes when you look at me."

"You think I'm wise?"

"I think you've got big pretty eyes."

Hands unsteady, she put the bundle of clothes in the laundry bag, then lifted her suitcase to the floor. She was in sad shape when having her eyes compared to an owl's made her hands shake. Primly she sat on the bed. "I've been thinking."

He rolled onto one side, his body distracting her—all bronzed skin, defined muscle, ripped abs, gorgeous legs. "Aw, darlin', didn't we decide you think too much?"

"Do you have any condoms?"

Now it was his turn to do the owl look. She kept her

gaze locked on his, refusing, however tempted, to check out any physical response he might have to the question. "I…uh…condoms…"

His cheeks turned deep bronze beneath his tan, and she marveled. Not only had she left him at a loss for words, she'd made him blush.

He cleared his throat. "As a matter of fact, I do."

"You never leave home without them. Is that it?"

"No. I mean, no, I don't always have them. I don't just assume that there's always going to be some woman who can't resist me." He shuffled the papers together and put them on the night table, then rolled to sit up. "I have them now because, uh, Alex always, uh, keeps them on the plane, and I took a couple, uh, just in case…"

She found comfort in his discomfort. He was as vulnerable about this sex business as she was, and that bolstered her confidence. "Because you figured eventually I wouldn't be able to resist you?"

The unease disappeared from his eyes, his expression turning serious and intense. "No, doc. I knew *I* couldn't resist *you*. As for you, I was…hopeful."

Hopeful. Just the word gave her a lovely tingle deep inside. To think that a man like Justin—obscenely wealthy, sinfully handsome and wickedly sexy—would *hope* for her… There were a million women prettier than her at home in his social world, better suited to him in every way, and he'd picked *her*.

For the time being, the insecurity in her reminded her.

At the moment, that was enough. Spending time with him, learning to like him and to trust him, maybe even falling in love with him—this was one of those opportunities Granddad had talked about, and she intended to make the best of it. If it didn't last, if the future she hoped for didn't come to pass, at least she would have the comfort of knowing she'd given it her best shot.

And if the Wallace brothers killed them in thirty-six hours, what did the future matter?

He was staring at her, his hands resting on his thighs, his bare feet almost toe to toe with her slippers. She wished she'd taken time to dry her hair. That she'd spritzed on a bit of perfume. That she'd packed something silky and sheer and incredibly sexy to put on so he could take it off.

As if she even owned anything silky, sheer and sexy. That wasn't who she was. This—damp hair, pajamas dotted with owls or kissing lips or flamingos, fuzzy pink slippers—this was who she was. Who he wanted.

A quick glance lower left no doubt of that.

Still, she hesitated. "Do you think it's terribly unromantic, talking this way?"

His mouth quirked. "Logic and reason can be romantic in their own way. I'd rather know you'd considered all the possible results and decided you wanted to do it anyway than that you got swept away by my boyish charm and regretted it tomorrow morning."

She sniffed. "Sometimes your charm is about on a par with a snake."

He took no offense but smiled the way a snake might in baring its fangs. That ability to shrug off her comments was one of the things she liked about him.

One of many.

Uncertainty claimed her again. She slipped off the fuzzy pinks, then dug her toes into the soles as she stood. Now what? Her first time with Trent had started with a kiss and ended on the floor in a jumble of clothes just short of her bed. Her first time with AJ and pretty much everyone in between had happened the same way.

Now that she'd talked the spontaneity right out of the situation...

Justin shut off the bedside lamp, then reached unerringly for her. His hands settled at her waist and drew her closer, tugging her down onto the mattress beside him. "Come here," he murmured, his mouth brushing hers. "I've been wanting to do this for a long time."

The sheets were warm where he'd lain, and more heat radiated from his body. She had a moment to think how good he smelled, wickedly expensive and sexy and masculine, then his mouth covered hers and all she could think was *good*. He loomed over her, his knees settling outside hers, and she slid her hands to his shoulders, then glided one hand into his hair while the other grazed his neck and the stubble of his jaw.

His skin was smooth, silken, hot, and it warmed her skin while his tongue heated her from the inside out. He was amazing to the touch, cervical vertebra one, two, three, trapezius muscle, scapula, thoracic one, two, three. She knew the parts of the body intimately, having studied, touched, repaired, dissected, but knowing *the* body had nothing on learning *Justin's* body. His was perfection. And for tonight, it was hers.

His kiss went on forever, slow, simmering, and she realized the spontaneity might be gone, but the anticipation was double. With each stroke of his tongue, each soft sound, each touch of her hands on him, the heat inside her flared higher, like a fire finding fresh bursts of oxygen everywhere it flickered. It licked along her skin, heated her blood, sucked the breath from her lungs and left her damp, aching, needing.

When his hands slid beneath her pajama top, cupping her breasts, his fingers finding her sensitive nipples, she gasped, the sound swallowed by his mouth. When her own greedy hands began shoving at his boxers, he did the same. He braced on trembling arms, never leaving her mouth, so she could push the fabric out of the way, then he kicked free and she wrapped her fingers around his erection. Swollen, straining, skin so soft and hot…

His hips arched away from her caresses, and finally he tore his mouth from hers. "Let me get…" His voice was barely recognizable: husky, thick, words brutally formed.

He shifted to the foot of the bed, where a zipper rasped loudly, followed by the crinkle of plastic. When he returned, he sat back on his heels, and in the dim light that came from the bathroom, his grin was satisfied and cocky and tender. For her. His fingers curled around the waistband of her pajamas, and she automatically lifted her hips to let him slide them and the thin cotton panties underneath down her legs. They landed somewhere behind him. While he watched, she curled her own fingers around the hem of the top and reversed the action.

"Aw, doc… You are beautiful."

"So are you." Tentatively she touched his hip, his rock-hard abdominal rectus muscle.

"Mark this day on the calendar. Dr. Cate Calloway gave me a compliment."

She took the condoms from his grip, tossed all but one on the nightstand, then ripped the package open. "She's going to do a whole lot more than just compliment you," she murmured. *"Now."*

With a laugh, he took the condom she offered and rolled it in place, his hands unsteady, then he pushed her back on the bed, leaning over her, making her feel warm and secure and safe and wanted. When he kissed her again, she thought she might have swooned, and when he entered her, stretching, filling her, everything inside her gave a great, satisfying sigh.

It felt so good. So perfect. So *right*.

Chapter 10

The insistent beeping of the alarm woke Justin before dawn the next morning, pinging louder and louder into his dream until he couldn't ignore it any longer. He didn't want to move, didn't want to give up the sweet heat of the body curled next to his, the sweet scent of the hair tangled beneath his chin, the incredibly sweet ease brought about by incredibly sweet sex. When he opened his eyes, the dream would disappear, so he kept them shut while swinging one hand out to find the offending clock and silence it.

Then the dream sighed softly and snuggled closer and, poof, he had the champion of morning erections, and the night before came flooding back to him. Cate. Underneath him, on top of him, cuddled against him. Shared kisses and caresses and orgasms and whispers.

He'd thought his entire life had been one of luck, but now he knew for real what getting lucky meant.

She stretched, touching every sensitive part he owned, which appeared to be everything, then sleepily slurred, "It's still dark. Do we have to get up?"

Get up? Let go of her, get out of bed, put on clothing? No. Hell, no. He'd waited too long for this moment— forever, he was pretty sure—to end it prematurely for... For what? Why had he set the damned alarm?

His brain was foggy. He hadn't slept enough, and those hours before sleep had been sensory overload. Not enough thinking and more feeling than he'd experienced in a lifetime. But before then, before Cate had come out of the shower looking adorably sexy and serious, when he'd set the alarm...

It came back to him with enough emotional punch to shrivel the most determined erection. Luisa. The pervert doctor. Keeping the Wallaces from killing Susanna and Trent.

He pressed a kiss to Cate's hair, then, when she stretched again, her cheek, her throat, her shoulder. She purred—Cate, whose only kittenish behavior toward him in the past had consisted of hissing and the baring of claws—and rolled to face him, sliding one arm around him.

"We've got to see what we can find about Luisa," he said, and instantly her eyes came open. He studied them for any hint of surprise that it was him she curved so intimately against, or regret that she'd given in to him in a weak moment.

But there was no oh-God-what-have-I-done in her blue eyes, just a sudden alertness that chased away the sleepiness, the dreaminess, but not the intimacy. She raised her hand, rubbing her fingers lightly over the day-old beard there. "I don't suppose we could be hiding when Dr. Sutton comes out to his car and pepper spray the truth out of him."

He twisted his head to kiss her knuckles. "I'd rather just beat it out of him with my fists."

"Are you much of a fighter?"

"What I lack in skill, I make up for with enthusiasm." Then he grinned. "I've won my share of fights. I've also had my ass kicked a few times."

"I never imagined Justin Seavers knew how to lose."

"I don't when it's important." And *she* was important.

Just like Luisa, Trent and Susanna, the renewed beeping reminded him. He must have hit Snooze instead of the Off button.

Cate sat up, as reluctant to move as he was to let her, then shut off the alarm. Her spine was straight, the skin soft and golden all the way down to the flare of her hips. He expected her to be shy, despite the fact he'd seen every bit of her last night, but she stood, shoved her feet into her slippers, grabbed a neatly folded set of clothes from her suitcase and disappeared into the bathroom.

He enjoyed every step of her journey.

While he waited, he dressed, located her pajamas and tossed them on her bed, threw away the empty condom wrappers and combed his fingers through his hair. He was antsy, wanting to get out to the Sutton place, to make sure the pervert doctor went to his office as usual and didn't take Luisa with him.

And if he didn't? If they got the chance to talk to her?

Cate returned, hair damp to tame the bedhead and wearing the jeans from last night with a long-sleeved T-shirt that clung in all the right places, along with the slippers. As she sat down on the bed to put on running shoes and socks, he asked, "What is it with you and the pink things? Do you have a phobia about walking bare-footed on motel carpet?"

Color tinged her cheeks. "It's not a phobia. It's just a personal preference."

"They're feet," he teased. "They're meant to get dirty."

"I like mine clean," she said primly.

Laughing, he took his turn in the bathroom. By the time he came back, she was waiting, purse and Garcia's files in one hand, their jackets in the other. Her pajamas were packed, the duffel holding her suitcase and his backpack on the floor at her feet. She followed his gaze to them and said, "Just in case."

In case they got lucky—or unlucky—and couldn't return to the motel. He nodded and hefted the bag over his shoulder.

The parking lot lights buzzed, auras forming around each lamp. If anyone was stirring in the other rooms, it was hard to tell. They put on their jackets to guard against the predawn chill, got into the car with its creaky, cold seats and made a stop at a fast-food drive-through before heading to the Sutton house.

Nothing had changed. Lights still blazed at the back, providing security for the animals, the SUV was still parked in the driveway and the house sat in darkness. Settled in at the same vantage point as the night before, they ate sausage biscuits and greasy hash browns, washing them down with coffee that provided caffeine and warmth, if not much in the way of flavor.

"Pediatricians don't do much surgery, do they?" he asked, as Cate gathered the wrappers and napkins, wadding them together in the bag.

"Generally not. That's what referrals are for."

"Would Sutton have patients in the hospital he'd want to see before work?"

She shrugged, hugging her arms across her middle. "It's hard to say. So many facilities have gone to the hospitalist system—staff doctors whose job is to oversee inpatient care, regardless of who the patient's primary doctor is. I'm guessing when he leaves here, he'll go straight to his office."

Which opened at 7:30 a.m. Divers weren't the only ones who had to get up and around early.

She looked uncomfortable and cold on the ground, so he shifted position until one of the boulders was against his back. "Come here."

The look she gave him was both wary and tempted. He made his answering look as innocent as possible. "I'm just offering you a place to sit where your ass doesn't freeze. Come on, Cate. We already played doctor half of last night. Surely you don't think I'm going to get fresh with you here."

"'Fresh'?" she mocked, but she moved across the stone to slide onto his lap. "That sounds like something my grandparents would say."

"It's something my grandparents *do* say." He wrapped his arms around her, and she settled against him. He'd offered to warm her, but just that contact sent heat blazing through *him*. "For filthy rich, they're good people."

She slanted him a look before resting her head on his shoulder. He couldn't blame her for having prejudices against people like his family. Trent had neglected her and been unfaithful. His parents hadn't warmed to her, either—his mother hadn't hidden her disappointment that her only son hadn't picked someone more *suitable*—and neither had his friends, and now the Wallaces wanted to kill her. It could give a woman an in-feriority complex.

"What are we going to do after Sutton leaves?"

"Try to talk to Luisa?" He shrugged. "We can't call the police. We don't have time."

"Do you think he'll leave her here alone all day, as young as she is?"

"Honey, they didn't adopt her. They *bought* her. They've kept her existence a secret. Apparently, she sleeps in the basement. I don't think he's going to worry about her being home alone. She's not going to call for help—she doesn't know anyone *to* call—and she's not going to run away because she doesn't have anywhere to go. Whatever's going on inside that house, at least she's got food, shelter and a place to sleep."

Cate snuggled a little closer and whispered, "She's got us."

He smiled thinly. If they could be of any use to her. The Wallaces could have already put out the word to all their customers: get rid of the kids, at least tempo-rarily. That could mean shipping them off somewhere, selling them to someone else or, if the so-called parents had enough to lose, killing them. Desperate people took desperate measures to avoid prison.

The Wallaces were desperate.

His butt was growing numb by the time they saw some activity across the road. Cate shifted to the ground, sinking out of sight, and he did the same. Sutton came out of the house, juggling a travel mug, a protein bar and his suit coat to lock the deadbolt behind him. He strode to the steps, beeping the electronic lock on the SUV, then climbed inside, turned in a U and headed toward the road.

He was in his midforties, excess pounds around his

middle and sparse hair on his head. He wore a smug, self-satisfied look, as if he were king of his realm, off to his practice in an upscale building, to treat the kids of parents who could afford his rates or had the insurance to cover them. He probably never did volunteer work, never treated a patient for free or, more, paid for the treatment himself, like Cate did. Sure, she called the supplies she shipped to La Casa donations, but Trent and Susanna knew she was the donor.

Sutton turned toward town, unaware that his kingdom was about to get shaken up.

"Bastard," Cate muttered. "Let's make sure he's gone, then go over and see if Luisa will talk to us."

Justin stood, then pulled her to her feet, deliberately tugging hard enough to pull her off balance and into his arms. She caught herself with both hands on his chest, giving him a chiding look.

"You're incorrigible."

He grinned. "But you adore me anyway, don't you?"

"You have enough ego for any ten men. I'm not adding to it." But she wrapped her fingers around his and held on until they reached the car.

They waited until ten minutes had passed, then he started the engine. On the short drive to the Sutton house, he figured what to say if Sutton returned for some reason—that he was hoping to talk to Mrs. Sutton about a horse. Based on Garcia's information, including the wife's blog that included tons of pictures of herself, dogs and horses and no mention of a husband or child, it didn't seem likely the doctor shared her four-legged passion.

"You stay here," he said when he parked where the SUV had been.

Cate paused in the act of unbuckling her seat belt. "We know Sutton's not here."

"But we don't know whether anyone else is. Presumably there are animals out back. Someone's got to take care of them while the wife is gone."

Scowling, she folded her hands in her lap.

Sliding out, he ducked back down to grin at her. "Thanks, doc. You know, I adore you, too."

That was a major understatement, he thought as he climbed the porch steps. Like saying diving was fun or Cozumel was nice.

The first picture window he passed opened into an office, dimly lit and empty, the door closed. Reaching the door, he rang the bell and listened to it echo inside. After the sound faded, he rang it again, then walked farther along the porch to the next window. The living room was also dimly lit, also empty. Everything looked immaculate—not a footprint on the carpet, tables gleaming, nothing obviously out of place.

It was a good housekeeping job for people who worked and didn't have a housekeeper.

When he shifted his gaze to the kitchen, a faint blur of movement caught his attention, nothing solid, just a shadow shifting on the wood floor. He crossed the porch in a few strides, gestured to Cate to wait, then circled to the rear of the house.

The porch there was identical to the one in front, though the boards were more worn. A path of paving stones led to the barn and kennels; a door opened into what was probably the dining part of the kitchen. Unlike the front door, this one had a window with red gingham curtains blocking the lower half of the glass. Above the fabric the dining room was visible—a scarred oak table with four heavy chairs, a hallway leading into shadow, a countertop separating the table from the '70s-era kitchen.

He rapped his knuckles on the wood. "Dr. Sutton? Mrs. Sutton?"

Utter silence was the only response.

Stepping closer to the door, he lowered his voice. "Luisa? Can you hear me? *¿Puedes oírme? Soy un amigo de Susanna.*"

More silence. Stillness.

"Luisa, *quiero ayudarle. Susanna y Trent me enviaron.*"

A creak on the steps made him whirl around, heart thudding, then sag against the doorjamb. "Sheesh, Cate, I thought you'd agreed to wait."

"I'm just checking on you. Is she here?"

"I'm talking. She's not answering. And all I've seen is maybe a shadow." He turned back to the door, his hand flattened on the frame. "Luisa, *por favor.* Susanna is worried about you. Everyone at La Casa is worried. We just want to know you're okay."

He listened a long time, straining for any sound besides his own breaths, but nothing came.

Finally Cate touched his arm. "She's afraid," she said softly. "You know she's been taught to stay out of sight."

"I know." His fingers curled into a fist. "Damn it! If Susanna were here… Luisa knows her. She trusts her."

Cate didn't state the obvious—if Susanna were free to be there, *they* wouldn't be there—and he appreciated it. But she did catch her breath and raised one trembling hand to point at the door. When he looked, his own breath caught in his chest.

Fragile fingers lifted one corner of the gingham curtain, and peering up at them through the glass, her expression one of bone-deep sadness tinged with the faintest bit of hopefulness, was Luisa.

Cate bent to the girl's level. "Hi, Luisa. I'm Cate, and this is Justin. Susanna asked us to come here and see if you're all right." She knew the girl spoke at least some English; Trent had surprised everyone by discovering a talent for teaching it. Just like everything else, he'd turned it into a game the girls had loved to play. "Can you open the door, sweetheart?"

After an intense stare, Luisa let the curtain drop. Before the fear that she'd run off to hide could register fully in Cate's brain, the lock clicked and the door slowly swung in.

"Where is Susanna?" the girl asked, peeking from behind the door. "Is she here?"

"She's in Cozumel. She sent us to see you. Is it okay if we talk to you?"

"The doctor won't like."

"But he's gone for the day, isn't he?" Cate eased inside before the girl could change her mind, sat down at the table and nudged another chair out for Luisa to sit in front of her. "The doctor... Is that your new daddy?"

Her small face wrinkled in distaste. "He's not my daddy, and she's not my mama. He's doctor and she's ma'am."

Cate gestured to Justin and he pulled out a third chair, drawing Luisa's attention his way while Cate studied her. "Everyone misses you at La Casa. They wonder how you like your new home. Do you like it?"

She vigorously shook her head. Besides the really bad haircut, her thin sleeveless dress was inadequate for the morning chill. The dress hung from her shoulders, while the cheap flip-flops on her feet pinched between her toes and left a sliver of heel hanging over the edge. She was about average height for her age group, but definitely underweight. Her arms and legs were like skinny sticks, and her right arm bore bruises in varying stages of healing and about the size of the paunchy doctor's pudgy fingers. More bruises were visible on her legs, and there was a stiffness to the way she held her left arm that suggested a previous injury.

Cate tuned back in to the conversation in time to hear Justin ask, "What do you do here?"

With an expression far too defeated for an eight-year-old, she replied, "I take care of the house. I vacuum. I sweep. I mop. I wash dishes. I cook. I do laundry. I make beds. I clean the commodes and scrub the bathtubs. I dust the tables and the statues and the pictures." She ticked them off on her fingers and ran out of fingers before chores.

"When do you start working?"

"When the sun comes up."

"And when are you usually done?"

"At bedtime."

"What do you eat?"

Luisa scrubbed one hand across her nose. "Ma'am keeps my food here." She went to the counter and opened the first door on the left. Inside was a jumbo jar of peanut butter, a loaf of bread and a bag of sugary cereal.

"You don't eat the food in the refrigerator?" Cate asked, the sausage biscuit and hash browns turning sour in her stomach.

The girl's eyes darted away as she vigorously shook her head. "No, never." The guilty gesture proclaimed she was lying.

Good for her, Cate thought fiercely. "Can we see your room where you sleep?"

Luisa hesitated, waiting for an encouraging nod from Justin to lead them down a short, shadowy hall. The utility room opened off the left; the door on the right went into the basement.

The space was huge and lit by several forty-watt bulbs, leaving deep shadows that made the skin on Cate's arms crawl. Luisa bypassed the clutter and storage and ducked through a door into a small, nearly empty room. The sight broke Cate's heart: a twin-size mattress on the floor with a sheet, a pillow and two blankets. A meager pile of neatly folded clothing stacked on the floor. A snapshot of Susanna, Trent and the staff at La Casa taped low on the wall so she could see it from the bed. A stuffed monkey with its fur rubbed thin from too much cuddling.

Cate's vision grew blurry. She'd bought that monkey last year, and three dozen other furry critters so the girls could each have a snuggle-baby, as her nieces called them, of her own.

"This is where you sleep, where you live." Justin's voice was vibrating with anger so harsh Cate would have had trouble recognizing it if she hadn't watched him speak.

"Yes." Luisa skipped across the room and carefully peeled the picture from the wall, then picked up the monkey and skipped back. "I'm ready to go now. I want to see Susanna."

Cate's gaze jerked to Justin. She was about to say, oh, no, they couldn't take her; they had to leave her here while the authorities figured things out, and he knew it. She could see it in the narrowing of his gaze. But she couldn't make the words come. Yes, it was kidnapping; yes, it was wrong. But more wrong than leaving an undernourished child showing signs of abuse in the hands of the people who starved and abused her?

Justin stepped close to her in the gloom and whispered, "Leverage, doc."

She gazed up at him bleakly. "Little girl," she whispered back. Feigning cheerfulness, she asked, "Do you have a jacket or a sweater, Luisa?"

"No. I don't go outside. I don't need one."

Justin slid out of his own jacket, then wrapped it around her before lifting her into his arms. His muscles didn't strain beneath her slight weight.

Abruptly the elephants started another performance in Cate's stomach. She was pretty sure there was some sort of law against talking their way into a stranger's house, and she knew for damn sure there was a law against taking a child away with them. What if they got to the top of the stairs and Sutton was waiting, or one of his wife's employees? What if one of the Wallaces' employees was waiting with a little .45-caliber leverage of his own?

She would claw his damn face off.

But there was no one at the top of the stairs. No one in the kitchen or on the back porch or in the driveway. Justin settled Luisa in the backseat of the rental, hastily fastening her seat belt, then he and Cate got in and buckled up. A thought occurred to her as he made a U-turn the way Sutton had, and she voiced it almost without concern. "You think they have a surveillance camera back there by the barn?"

"Doesn't matter. Sutton will call the Wallaces, and the Wallaces will know it's us."

Just in case, she waved in the direction of the barn. A one-fingered wave that didn't begin to express the disgust she felt for the Suttons.

They were practically to the highway, Justin grim and silent, Luisa eagerly watching the scenery pass. *I don't go out outside,* she'd said. Everything seemed new and unfamiliar to her. The panic that had threatened back at the house erupted in Cate's chest, constricting her lungs, twitching her nerves and muscles in an anxious spasm. She bent forward, hugging herself tightly, struggling for breath, and Justin spared one hand from the steering wheel to touch her shoulder.

"You all right, doc?"

She glanced at Luisa, still distracted by the view, then frantically whispered, "We've *kidnapped* a child!" Granted, Luisa didn't legally belong to the Suttons, but it would take time for the authorities to sort that out and they likely wouldn't be willing to let Cate and Justin go on their way while they did so.

Justin grinned. *Grinned.* "And you say you're not a risk taker. When you decide to break the rules, you do it in a big way, don't you?" He turned onto the interstate access ramp and revved the engine to make a smooth merge into the lane. "Don't think *kidnap,* Cate. Think *rescued.* Sounds a lot better, doesn't it?"

She looked at Luisa again, so thin, her little shoulders sagging under the responsibility she'd borne for months. *Rescued.* Yes, they'd rescued her from a life as the Suttons' own personal slave. The distinction might not make much difference in court, but it was good for her. It was enough to ease her breathing.

Their first stop was another fast-food drive-through to get breakfast for Luisa. She couldn't decide between biscuits and pancakes and a hamburger, so Justin ordered all three, and while they sat in the parking lot, the girl ate until Cate could see her belly distend beneath the thin dress.

"First we get her clothes and shoes that fit," Justin said quietly, as she munched. "I'll call Alex's pilots and tell them to be ready to take off as soon as we get to the airport."

"And then you call the Wallaces and tell them...?"

"We've got the files and we want to move up the trade to tonight."

"Where?"

"Trent's cousin Rick... You said he's in Atlanta."

Cate nodded, relief shivering through her that *finally* they were bringing in someone trained to deal with criminals. Finally, please, God, they could do so without getting anyone killed.

"Then that's where we'll go."

"Do you think they'll agree to the change?"

"They want those files back, I suspect the sooner the better." His gaze flickered to Luisa. "The sooner we get Trent and Susanna back in the U.S., the better. Preferably before Sutton finds out she's gone."

Sutton would be livid at losing his six-figure investment. The brothers wouldn't be pleased, either, at the possibility of their adoption scam collapsing like dominoes. The loss of all that money. The prospect of all those years in prison. They would come prepared to kill everyone.

If they came at all. They might send Trent and Susanna. They would definitely send their thugs. But Joseph and Lucas themselves might well direct their own private plane to the nearest country without an extradition agreement.

"Okay," she said, then breathed deeply. Tonight, no later than tomorrow, this ordeal would be over. Trent and Susanna would be free or dead. So would she and Justin. And if they survived? They would continue to see each other…or not. Her theory that this attraction was just a side effect of a dangerous situation, though it didn't feel that way anymore, might be proven right. Justin's claim that near-death experiences didn't make him commit to the first woman he saw, that she was special, might be proven instead.

They might wind up with the happily-ever-after that she really wanted. Or he might break her heart.

But she wouldn't have any regrets.

They made a fast sweep through a discount clothing store, Cate selecting a complete wardrobe, at least for a few days, for Luisa while Justin contacted Alex's pilot. After a rushed drive to the airport, they were on board the Gulfstream and airborne by the time she caught her breath.

Justin didn't bother with the phone number the oily guy had given Cate, but placed his call directly to Lucas Wallace in his Gulfport, Mississippi, office. While Luisa was occupied by the big-screen television, Justin sprawled back in a chair, looking as if he had nothing more important on his mind than enjoying the flight and sounding it, too.

"Hey, Luke, it's Justin Seavers."

Cate leaned close to hear the other end of the conversation. For a moment there was nothing but the sound of tension on the line, then Wallace said in a phony, cheery voice, "Justin. It's been a long time."

"Not long enough, buddy. There's been a change of plans."

"What plans?"

"Tomorrow's trade. We want to do it tonight. In Atlanta. Tell your people to have Trent and Susanna there by this evening. I'll call you—"

"Whoa, hang on. I don't know what you're talking about. What plans? Where are Trent and Susanna?"

Justin's smile was feral. "Considering you've been a lying son of a bitch your whole worthless life, you don't play innocent well. We've got your files, and we want Trent and Susanna tonight, not tomorrow. I'll call you back with a time and place. You'd damn well better have them there, or we send the files to every media outlet north *and* south of the border."

Without waiting for a response, he pressed the End button, then offered the phone to Cate. The smile was gone. Good, because it had made her shiver. Now his expression was merely intent. "Call Trent's cousin."

It took one call to get the office number, another to connect. "Special Agent Calloway," Rick said in a distracted drawl.

Her fingers were unsteady, her heart pounding, and she had to swallow to get words out, but her voice sounded pretty normal, she thought. At least for the circumstances. "Rick, it's Cate Calloway. I'm on my way to Atlanta, and I need to see you."

He must have been surprised—she only saw him on occasion when he was visiting family in Copper Lake—but it didn't show in his response. "Hey, Cate, what's up?"

She cleared her throat, glanced at Justin and took a breath when he nodded. "Quite a bit, actually. Trent's been taken hostage in Cozumel, and I've kidnapped an eight-year-old girl. Do you think you can fit me into your schedule?"

Chapter 11

Cate must have felt as if she were back in medical school, an annoying little bug who couldn't say a single word that didn't draw scorn from the men seated around them at the table. Justin sat beside her, and Luisa stood fearfully at his shoulder, watching wide-eyed. He wasn't sure how much the girl understood, but she was expert at matching tones to unpleasant memories.

"Let's get this straight," the FBI guy said. "Trent Calloway and his girlfriend have been missing for *five days* and you just now get around to telling us."

"Not missing," Cate said coolly. "Held hostage. We didn't call because, gee, when men with guns shoot at you, then tell you 'don't call the police,' it seems like a good idea to not call the police."

"And now you want us to...what? Haul your butts out of this mess?"

The look she gave FBI guy was even frostier than

her voice. "No, I trusted our butts to Rick and GBI. I didn't call you."

Rick Calloway, an older, tougher version of Trent, raised one hand. "I had to bring the FBI in, Cate. We're talking interstate and international child trafficking. Like it or not, a good part of it's their jurisdiction."

FBI guy scrubbed his hand through his thinning hair. "Just my luck I'm on call when the amateurs come out to play."

"Shut up, Madden," the third man at the table said. He was GBI, as well, and looked like he'd slept in a refrigerator box the last few months. His hair was dark and wild; so was his beard. But his eyes were as clear and sharp as ice. Rick had called him Evan; after his first scornful look, FBI guy hadn't spoken to him at all.

"Hey, don't tell me—"

Evan stopped FBI guy with a look. He might as well have had *Doesn't play well with others* tattooed on his forehead. Justin would rather have just one of him on their side than two dozen FBI guys.

FBI guy scrubbed his hair again, then dropped his hand to his stomach. "I'm gonna get some coffee."

When the conference room door closed behind him, Rick laughed. "Evan has a reputation for being right on the edge of crazy insane. People are leery of working with him." But not him. He treated him like a buddy.

The man gave no hint he heard the words.

Rick settled his gaze on Cate. "I have to say, I would've expected Trent to get into trouble long before you. You've always been the responsible one."

"You did notice I wouldn't be in this trouble if not for Trent. Let's talk before that idiot comes back. You know, for five days, virtually every man I've dealt with has been a jerk. It doesn't speak highly of your gender." Then she blinked. "Present company excluded, of course."

"She means you guys," Justin said. "I've been a jerk."

She looked at him, and a small smile touched her lips. She even scooted her chair a little closer. Luisa ducked into the space between them, one hand on Cate's arm, the other on his.

"What about Luisa?" Cate asked.

"We'll leave her here with a couple of agents."

Luisa began shaking her head. "No, no. I want to see Susanna." Dark eyes pleading, she looked from Cate to Justin, then grasped his hand in both of hers. "*Quiero ver a Susanna. Quiero ir a casa—La Casa. Por favor,* Justin!"

He lifted her into his lap and smoothed her hair back, cupping his hands to her cheeks. "Luisa, we'll be back, I promise, and we'll bring Susanna with us. It'll be just a few hours. They'll get supper for you, whatever you want, and you can watch TV, and then Susanna will come."

Her lip stopped quavering, and the fear lessened in her eyes. "A few hours?"

"Yes."

"Two hours?"

"Maybe three. You might even fall asleep before we get back."

"But you will bring Susanna and Trent?"

"Yes."

She stared at him a long time, then sagged against him with a weary whisper. "Okay."

His stomach knotted. Those were some awfully big promises. But he didn't make promises he couldn't keep. With the GBI's assistance—and a lot from God—they were going to walk out of the meeting tonight, alive and well: Trent, Susanna, Cate and him. They would all be safe to go back to their normal lives, Susanna and Trent at La Casa, and he and Cate…

He and Cate didn't *have* a normal life yet. But they would. Just because this crisis was nearly over didn't mean they were. They wouldn't be. Not ever.

"Okay," Rick said. "Our teams are set up at the hangar. Justin, you'll be wearing that under your shirt."

The hangar was abandoned in a little-used area of the airport. The Wallaces could taxi their jet right inside and close the doors behind them, except that Rick's guys had disabled the doors and brought in some junked equipment and crates to provide themselves with cover.

Wondering what kind of cover he'd have, Justin followed Rick's gesture to the bulletproof vest at the other end of the table, and his stomach knotted again. Being shot at when he didn't expect it was one thing; being prepared for getting shot at again was another entirely. He liked risk and excitement, yeah, but he wasn't a hero. For the first time in five days, this was *real*. He felt it in every one of his cowardly bones.

"Where's mine?" Cate asked.

He snorted and said the same thing at the same time as Rick. "You're not going in."

"Wait a minute. They brought me into this. I didn't volunteer. They'll expect me to be there."

"You'll be in the car," Evan said. "If they want to see you, you can roll the window down. But you're not getting out."

"Why? Because I'm a woman?"

"Because it's easier to protect one target than two." Evan flashed what probably passed for a smile. "Don't worry. I'll be in the car with you."

Cate didn't argue, but Justin knew not to assume she

was accepting their decision. "You'd better handcuff her to the steering wheel. She's very stubborn about not doing what she's told." Then he grinned, probably doing as poorly a job of it as Evan did. "Besides, we might need an E.R. doc by the time we're done. If you need to apply pressure to me, you know the places I like it best."

She tried to glare at him, but after a moment she just rolled her eyes and shook her head.

Rick's phone beeped, and he pulled it out. "I don't know which of you pissed off Madden most, but it looks like he's going to text rather than come back in here. The Wallaces' private jet took off from Cozumel an hour ago. Destination Atlanta. We'd better get out to the hangar. Traffic the way it is, they could beat us there."

While Evan helped Justin with the vest, Rick called a female agent to take charge of Luisa. She hugged both him and Cate, made him promise again that he'd bring back Susanna, then left the room with the woman.

"The faith of a child," Cate murmured.

He tugged his T-shirt back in place. "Do you have faith in me?"

"I do." Simple. Solemn. More gratifying than any two words should ever be.

He bent close, brushing her ear with his mouth. "You're gonna say that to me at least one more time, doc. You might as well start accepting it now."

She gave him a sweet, womanly smile that damn near took his breath away, then matter-of-factly said, "We'll talk about it."

His groan was only half-fake. Look at all the talking it had taken her to make love with him, and that was for a very important, granted, but small commitment. How much more would it take to get a lifetime commitment out of her?

They had filed out of the conference room and down the hall to the elevator when his cell phone rang. He checked the screen, ready to automatically mute the call, but the number there stopped him. Everyone around him went silent as he raised the phone to his ear, including the woman with Luisa, paused in the act of going through a doorway. "Hello, Joey."

"We want the girl."

Sweat popped out on Justin's forehead. "What girl?"

"You don't play stupid well, Seavers. We want the Suttons' kid. If she's not at the meeting, you've blown your last chance. You'll be taking your buddy Trent and his girlfriend home in caskets."

"You really think I'm dragging an eight-year-old kid around with me?"

"I really think you'd better have her at the hangar when I get there."

"Our deal was for the files."

"Now it's for the files *and* the girl."

"Why? Sutton was careless enough to lose her, so you're gonna give her back?"

Wallace's laugh was spook-house creepy. "Of course not. We have a number of prospective parents on our waiting list. We'll place her in another happy home."

"And collect another couple hundred grand in the process?" Justin's jaw clenched. "Your mother should have drowned both you and your brother at birth."

"Right back at you, Seavers. Bring the girl or lose your friends. Your choice."

"Bastard," Justin muttered. He shoved the phone back in his pocket. "I guess Sutton gets home early on Fridays."

He turned to look at Luisa, and so did everyone else.

"What the hell do we do now?"

* * *

It surprised Cate that just a few miles away, all the hustle and activity of a major city airport was taking place while here, in this little corner, all was still. The only light shining on the hangar, besides their own headlights, came from too-distant flood lamps that cast a lot of shadows but offered little illumination. The structure was big, peeling paint and showing rust, and she couldn't help but imagine it as the centerpiece of a slasher movie.

Justin slowed even more as he approached the entrance. "Wouldn't this make a great haunted house? The Crash of the Damned, Flight 4377. That's hell spelled upside down in numbers, you know. Fog and wind machines, an old fuselage, ripped metal and the ghosts of the passengers flitting about."

She shuddered. "Please tell me you do haunted houses at the community center and that's why your brain works along those lines."

"We do haunted houses at the community center." He spoke with utter seriousness until a grin broke it. "I'm not sure why my brain works the way it does."

He drove through the door practically at a crawl, circled around, then parked the borrowed SUV near the rear of the building. His gaze flickered to the rearview mirror. "Okay, we're inside. Now what?"

From the cargo area of the truck, Evan answered. "Leave the lights on, go over and flip the power switch on the west wall. Then come back, shut off the lights and the engine."

Dark as he was and dressed all in black, Cate couldn't identify any part of him when she glanced back as if checking on Luisa. She'd seen the guns he'd brought with him, though, high-tech, high-power, scary-looking weapons. Scarier, she hoped, than the Wallaces'.

Justin got out, the truck dinging, and followed Evan's instructions. She expected a blaze of bright lights, but the naked bulbs did little to dispel the darkness. She supposed since there were people hiding in the hangar, darkness was good, since she couldn't spot any of them, either.

From the backseat came a soft, frightened voice. *"¿Dónde está Susanna?"*

"Ella vendrá pronto," Evan responded.

Seemed everyone spoke Spanish except Cate. She should take classes…or ask Justin to teach her. As long as the first word he taught her wasn't *adiós*.

"Now what?" Justin rested his arms on the window frame, his hands loosely clasped. Tension radiated from him in waves…or was that her own tension bouncing off and reflecting back on her? He didn't *look* nervous, while she was so anxious she thought she might empty her stomach any moment.

"We wait," Evan replied with the patience of a man who'd done a lot of waiting in his life. "They'll let us know when the jet lands."

Justin came around to the passenger side and opened the door, tugging Cate out. The interior light, controlled by a switch on the dash, didn't come on—another handy feature, along with the heavily tinted windows. At the back of the building, between the truck and the exterior aluminum wall, no one could see them besides Luisa and Evan, and she'd bet he wasn't looking.

Turning so he leaned against the vehicle, Justin wrapped his arms around her from behind and pulled her snugly against him. The rigidity of the bulletproof vest discomforted her, but the rest of his body was achingly familiar. "We're almost there, doc. It's almost over."

She gripped his wrists, his radial pulse pounding

beneath one fingertip. He wasn't as calm as he looked. "I'm scared."

"So am I." He rested his chin on her head. "God, it's been one hell of a week. When this is done, we need a vacation. You, me, a yacht in the Caribbean..."

A week ago, she would have scoffed at the idea of going anywhere with Justin or splurging on the luxury of a yacht. Her only vacations included volunteer work, and even if she could have afforded a yacht, she couldn't have stopped thinking how much good that money could do elsewhere. Now... "That sounds wonderful."

He nuzzled her ear, bringing a shiver. "You realize, of course, that there are pirates all over the Caribbean."

She did scoff then. "After the Wallaces, pirates don't scare me."

A sharp rap on the rear side window drew their attention out the hangar doors. In the distance, a plane was taxiing their way, its lights small and insignificant in the night.

Justin pivoted her around. "Do everything Evan tells you, okay? Don't be stubborn. Don't try to stand with me. Just stay where you are. Okay?"

She felt as if she'd bitten into a lemon, her teeth grinding, the masseter muscles aching with the dismay of giving the answer he wanted. "Okay."

His gaze searched hers a moment, then he nodded, helped her back into the truck, and walked to the other side. He stopped about a dozen feet away, where he would be clearly visible to the passengers once the plane stopped, standing at an angle so she—and, more important, Evan—had a partial view of his face.

"Don't put your seat belt on," Evan said when she reached for it. "Get back out and stand on your side of the truck. Let them see you, but don't step out from behind the truck unless you have no other choice. And if things go wrong, duck."

She let the belt slide free and did as he said, unsure her legs were steady enough to hold her without Justin there for support. All she could have at the moment was a glance from him, along with a smile that flattened his mouth, but it would have to be enough.

Five days. This was only the fifth day since she'd left home, planning a pleasant, quiet trip, doing preventive care for the girls at the home and indulging in a little private envy of Trent and Susanna's relationship. Only five days, and so much had changed—her outlook, her life, her self. She was a different woman.

In love with a very different man.

The growl of the plane's engines grew louder as the pilot headed straight toward the hangar. At what seemed the last possible moment, the jet pivoted in a tight right turn, stopping so the exit was just outside the reach of the dim lights inside.

The door opened, the steps folded down, and two men, both armed, exited the plane and took up position on either side. The third man, Cate was sure, was the bastard she'd spoken to on the phone. He looked exactly the way he sounded: smarmy, phony, capable of horrible things. Evil in a thousand-dollar suit.

Followed by evil in a five-thousand-dollar suit. Cate recognized Joseph Wallace from fundraising brochures for La Casa—handsome, a little too polished. She'd always thought that veneer hid the superiority people like him—like Justin—wore to hide their contempt for those beneath them. Now she knew it hid the malevolence inside him.

And she whispered a silent apology to Justin for ever considering him equal to the snake.

Wallace stopped a dozen feet in front of Justin and gave him a sweeping look that dismissed him as harmless. "You have the files?"

Justin produced the flash drive from his pocket but didn't offer it.

"And the girl?"

"She's in the truck." Not quite turning his head, he called in Spanish, and Luisa leaned forward to wave one hand out the driver's window. "Where are Trent and Susanna?"

"In the plane. Get her out."

Justin grinned. "You show me yours and I'll show you mine."

Wallace hesitated, then gestured, and the smarmy guy walked back to the plane, leaning inside to bark a command. Cate's breath caught in her chest as she stared hard at the narrow door, waiting, willing, praying.

Susanna stepped out first, her hair curling wildly, her clothes rumpled, an air of utter exhaustion about her. She didn't appear to have been harmed, just very frightened. Still very frightened.

A few steps behind her was Trent, in jeans and a T-shirt, unshaven, also tired, but if he was afraid, like Justin, he hid it well.

From inside the truck, Cate heard Luisa squeal with delight at the sight of Susanna, and Evan whispered harshly to her, dissuading her, Cate guessed, from jumping out of the truck and running to her friend.

The guards stopped Susanna and Trent before they'd taken more than a few steps, and Wallace said, as politely bored as if he were ordering coffee and a pastry, "The flash drive and the girl."

Justin didn't move. "What if I made a copy of the files?"

Wallace shrugged. "We have instant access to the girls—all of them. If you create any further trouble, the results for them would be disastrous. Collateral damage. One of the costs of doing business."

To say nothing of the fact that he intended to have his thugs kill them all where they stood, Cate thought.

"That's a lot of valuable property to destroy," Justin said mildly.

Wallace's laugh sent a chill through her, forcing her to lean against the fender to stay upright.

"Maybe I was wrong earlier. You weren't playing stupid. You really are. Do you have any idea how many little girls there are in the world that nobody wants? I could replace these twenty-two with two hundred twenty-two in no time, and I'd have buyers clamoring for every one." He gestured again, and the men with guns came closer. Two more exited the plane.

When were Rick and Evan going to step in? It seemed the moment the plane's door had opened would have been a good time, or any second since then. Right now Cate would be happy to see the crabby FBI agent or even an airport security guard—anyone with a gun. "What are you waiting for?" she whispered.

She startled when Evan answered. "He just admitted to selling the kids. Anytime now."

Of course. A rich man like Joseph Wallace could buy the best defense ever. The more evidence, the stronger the case. Rick's team had set up cameras and were filming the exchange. What juror could watch Wallace talk so callously about selling and killing little girls and not convict him?

"My property, please," Wallace said, and Justin finally moved, walking forward to set the flash drive on top of a wooden crate halfway between them.

"And the girl."

"Since you sold her to the Suttons, isn't she technically their property?"

"Technically, I suppose. But if they can't control an eight-year-old, I'll find a buyer who can." Impatience shimmered in his next words. "Quit talking and get her out here. I've got a meeting in the morning regarding the children's home we're opening in El Salvador next month. I predict we'll be able to make a large number of placements with clients—er, parents—eager to bring grateful children into their lives."

"Of course you wouldn't want to miss that," Justin grumbled as he started toward the SUV.

"Okay," Evan murmured from inside the truck, and a soft thud sounded as he tossed a set of hearing protection ear muffs into the passenger seat.

Cate picked them up, her gaze darting from Justin, looking grim but relieved, to Evan, hastily putting an oversize pair of protectors onto Luisa. As Justin opened the door, he gave her a wink and a lazy grin, with a subtle backward nod.

She stepped a few feet to the right, the movement enough to catch Trent's attention, and fitted the thick padded cups over her ears. He murmured to Susanna, and both of them clamped their hands over their own ears as Justin lifted Luisa out of the backseat and turned, holding her head tightly to his chest and squeezing his eyes shut.

Even with protection, the explosion from the flashbang grenade Evan tossed through the open door was deafening. The blinding light jagged across Cate's eyelids as the noise reverberated from one wall to the other and back again. She sank to her knees, vaguely aware of shouts, movement, but all she could see for the time it took her eyes to readjust was brilliant light; all she could hear were echoes.

When hands touched her, her eyes popped open and she ripped off the ear cups. Justin pulled her into his arms, holding her tightly, and kissed her hard and fast. "Are you okay?"

She nodded. "Are you?"

He grimaced. "I can't hear you." It had been impossible for him to use hearing protection; even earplugs could have alerted Wallace and his men. His ears were going to be ringing for a while.

She cupped her hands to his face and stared intently into his beautiful brown eyes. "It's over, we're alive and I love you."

The grin that curved his mouth came slowly but was full of every bit of smug confidence she'd ever seen in him. "I know." Then he grew serious. "I love you, too."

"I know." She might not have acknowledged it, might have tried to give him every out in the book, but deep inside she knew. Some things weren't logical or predictable. Some things couldn't be thought through. Some things she just had to accept. Like getting shot at. Fleeing a foreign country. Rescuing friends from bad guys. Saving the world—at least for a few people.

And falling in love with the last guy in the world she would have picked for herself.

The only one she would trust with her happily-ever-after.

Snuggling deeper into his embrace, she gave him a sly look. "About that vacation you mentioned…"

It took a few days in Atlanta to tie things up, then Justin and Cate left for that vacation. He'd borrowed

Alex's plane again, and they'd flown back to Cozumel, catching a cab at the airport.

"Where are we going?"

He cocked his head to gaze at her. On the surface, they looked like opposites. He sprawled in the seat, too lazy to bother straightening his spine. She sat primly, spine erect, incredible legs crossed. His khaki shorts and Hawaiian shirt were rumpled from being stuffed in the first available space in the bag, and while he had shaved, he wasn't sure he'd remembered to comb his hair. Her shorts and shirt were neatly pressed, her hair braided without a strand out of place.

Delicate and sweeter than sugar most of the time— that had been Trent's description of her. Justin wondered how his buddy could have been so wrong about the woman he'd married. She wasn't delicate; she was strong, tough, resilient. And while she had her moments of sweetness, there was plenty of temper and stubbornness to offset it. She had a lot of buttons to push.

And he truly enjoyed pushing them.

"Someplace special," he said at last.

"Your house?"

He shook his head.

"La Casa?"

"Nope."

"A pier at which we'll find a luxurious yacht waiting to sail us away?"

"Nope." Actually, he did have that yacht waiting. He'd arranged a crew to handle the boat, but no chef or anyone else. He would take care of the cooking—the leasing agent was stocking the galley today—and cleaning up after themselves was a small price to pay for privacy.

The cabdriver turned onto a narrow street, a horn blaring from the car he'd narrowly avoided, but Cate held Justin's gaze. Slowly she smiled. "You know, I wouldn't let just anyone make plans for me, then not tell me."

"I know. But you trust me." He grinned his most obnoxious grin. "You said so, and I've got witnesses."

She twined her fingers with his. "The fact that I'm here proves I trust you. I don't care where we go, as long as we go together."

"Aw, doc, that's the sappiest thing you've ever said to me." He forced the words out around the sudden tightness in his chest. He didn't have a clue how Trent had failed to appreciate what he'd had in Cate, but he was damned grateful for it. He was going to be grateful every day that she loved him, and he was going to make her grateful that he loved her.

Except, of course, for the times she wanted to claw his face off.

After a few blocks, she sighed. "I'm glad it's over."

"Me, too." *Over* being relative. Joseph Wallace and the men who'd accompanied him Friday night were in jail, facing a boatload of charges including child trafficking and kidnapping. All twenty-two girls had been removed from their homes and placed in temporary foster care; eighteen sets of adoptive parents were taken into custody; warrants had been issued for the remaining four pairs; and the feds were hacking away at the computer files. Justin was pretty sure Garcia would decrypt them first.

Mexican authorities had been busy, too, arresting some of the Wallace Foundation staff members, everyone associated with the adoption agency and some local thugs on the Wallace payroll. The only major player who'd avoided jail so far was Lucas Wallace. While Joseph had gone to Atlanta to face Justin—and the cops—Lucas had boarded his own private jet for parts unknown. It appeared he'd taken twenty or thirty million dollars with him. Not a bad bankroll for a man on the run.

But the kids were okay, at least on the surface, and love could heal any resulting problems. Thanks to intervention by Trent's father, Luisa had been placed in the temporary custody of the woman in Idaho whose attempts to adopt her had put this whole ordeal in motion. Trent and Susanna were okay, too, spending a few days with her family before heading to Georgia to visit his family. All of them, including Justin and Cate, would have to testify at the upcoming trials, but he wasn't going to worry about that. With the delays Wallace's attorney would request, he and Cate would be celebrating at least their fifth anniversary before they had to set foot in a courtroom.

"I'm glad you and I weren't arrested for kidnapping Luisa."

Justin grinned at her. "Rescuing, doc. Keep the terminology straight. We saved Luisa's life." Again his chest grew uncomfortably tight, and his voice sounded rough. "I know you save lives all the time, but this was a first for me."

Her fingers tightened on his even as her smile gentled. "That's not true. You save lives with your time and your money. You help feed and shelter these girls. You give the kids at the community center opportunities they've never had. You give them hope. No one can live without hope." Leaning across the seat, she whispered, "You give me hope," then kissed him.

As usual, his body turned hot in the space of a breath, all the laziness he'd been experiencing earlier evaporating in a puff of smoke. Dimly he was aware of the cab slowing, turning, creeping so that the movement was barely perceptible. A scrape of metal was underscored by a mutter from the driver, but he didn't care. As long as they got some privacy in the next few minutes before *he* evaporated in a puff of smoke.

Finally, the car stopped and the driver cleared his throat. Cate broke the kiss, pulling back, giving him an intimate smile, before she primly turned her attention to picking up her purse, undoing the seat belt, opening the door.

"Oh." Her voice was soft and pleasantly surprised as she recognized their location. She gave him another intimate, bold, promise-of-pleasure smile as she got out of the car.

Justin paid the cabdriver, adding a generous tip for the scrapes, then hefted the duffel over his shoulder as the door to Room 11 opened.

"Tio Pablo!" Cate hugged the old man as if he were family, then breezed into the room where she and Justin had spent their first night together. "It's so good to be back."

Tio Pablo gave her a grin and Justin a wink. "It's good to have you back." He gestured toward a tray on the dresser. "Water, my best tequila, limes, a little Mayan avocado. What else do you need, besides time alone?"

Cate set her purse down, then slid her arm around Justin's waist before she answered. "Not a thing."

And he was in complete agreement. Drink, food and time with the most incredible woman he'd ever known. He didn't need a damn thing more.

* * * * *

COMING NEXT MONTH from Harlequin®
Romantic Suspense
AVAILABLE JULY 24, 2012

#1715 CAVANAUGH RULES
Cavanaugh Justice
Marie Ferrarella
Two emotionally closed-off homicide detectives take a chance on love while working a case together.

#1716 BREATHLESS ENCOUNTER
Code X
Cindy Dees
A genetically enhanced hero on a mission to draw out modern-day pirates rescues the woman who may actually be their target.

#1717 THE REUNION MISSION
Black Ops Rescues
Beth Cornelison
A black ops soldier and the woman who once betrayed him confront their undeniable attraction while he guards her and a vulnerable child in a bayou hideaway.

#1718 SEDUCING THE COLONEL'S DAUGHTER
All McQueen's Men
Jennifer Morey
It's this operative's mission to bring a kidnapped woman home. Will the headstrong daughter of a powerful colonel take his heart when he does?

You can find more information on upcoming Harlequin® titles, free excerpts and more at www.Harlequin.com.

HRSCNM0712

REQUEST YOUR FREE BOOKS!
2 FREE NOVELS PLUS 2 FREE GIFTS!

 Harlequin®

ROMANTIC
SUSPENSE

Sparked by Danger, Fueled by Passion.

YES! Please send me 2 FREE Harlequin® Romantic Suspense novels and my 2 FREE gifts (gifts are worth about $10). After receiving them, if I don't wish to receive any more books, I can return the shipping statement marked "cancel." If I don't cancel, I will receive 4 brand-new novels every month and be billed just $4.49 per book in the U.S. or $5.24 per book in Canada. That's a saving of at least 14% off the cover price! It's quite a bargain! Shipping and handling is just 50¢ per book in the U.S. and 75¢ per book in Canada.* I understand that accepting the 2 free books and gifts places me under no obligation to buy anything. I can always return a shipment and cancel at any time. Even if I never buy another book, the two free books and gifts are mine to keep forever.

240/340 HDN FEFR

Name	(PLEASE PRINT)	
Address		Apt. #
City	State/Prov.	Zip/Postal Code

Signature (if under 18, a parent or guardian must sign)

Mail to the **Reader Service:**
IN U.S.A.: P.O. Box 1867, Buffalo, NY 14240-1867
IN CANADA: P.O. Box 609, Fort Erie, Ontario L2A 5X3

Not valid for current subscribers to Harlequin Romantic Suspense books.

Want to try two free books from another line?
Call 1-800-873-8635 or visit www.ReaderService.com.

* Terms and prices subject to change without notice. Prices do not include applicable taxes. Sales tax applicable in N.Y. Canadian residents will be charged applicable taxes. Offer not valid in Quebec. This offer is limited to one order per household. All orders subject to credit approval. Credit or debit balances in a customer's account(s) may be offset by any other outstanding balance owed by or to the customer. Please allow 4 to 6 weeks for delivery. Offer available while quantities last.

Your Privacy—The Reader Service is committed to protecting your privacy. Our Privacy Policy is available online at www.ReaderService.com or upon request from the Reader Service.

We make a portion of our mailing list available to reputable third parties that offer products we believe may interest you. If you prefer that we not exchange your name with third parties, or if you wish to clarify or modify your communication preferences, please visit us at www.ReaderService.com/consumerschoice or write to us at Reader Service Preference Service, P.O. Box 9062, Buffalo, NY 14269. Include your complete name and address.

HRS11R

ROMANTIC
SUSPENSE

CINDY DEES

takes you on a wild journey to find the truth
in her new miniseries

Code X

Aiden McKay is more than just an ordinary man. As part of
an elite secret organization, Aiden was genetically enhanced
to increase his lung capacity and spend extended time under
water. He is a committed soldier, focused and dedicated
to his job. But when Aiden saves impulsive free spirit
Sunny Jordan from drowning she promptly overturns his
entire orderly, solitary world.

As the danger creeps closer, Adien soon realizes Sunny is the
target…but can he save her in time?

Breathless Encounter

Find out this August!

plus
BONUS
STORY
INSIDE!

Look out for a reader-favorite bonus story included in each
Harlequin Romantic Suspense book this August!

www.Harlequin.com

HRS27786

Werewolf and elite U.S. Navy SEAL, Matt Parker, must se *aside his prejudices and partner with beautiful Fae Sienn* *McClare to find a magic orb that threatens to expose the* *secret nature of his entire team.*

Harlequin® Nocturne presents *the debut of beloved author Bonnie Vanak's* *new miniseries,* PHOENIX FORCE.

Enjoy a sneak preview of THE COVERT WOLF, *available August 2012 from Harlequin® Nocturne.*

Sienna McClare was Fae, accustomed to open air an fields. Not this boxy subway car.

As the oily smell of fear clogged her nostrils, she inhale deeply, tried thinking of tall pines waving in the wind, the cha ter of birds and a deer cropping grass. A wolf watching a dee waiting. Prey. Images of fangs flashing, tearing, wet sounds..

No!

She fought the panic freezing her blood. And was gradu ally able to push the fear down into a dark spot deep insid her. The stench of Draicon werewolf clung to her like chea perfume.

Sienna hated glamouring herself as a Draicon werewol but it was necessary if she was going to find the Orb c Light. Someone had stolen the Orb from her colony, th Los Lobos Fae. A Draicon who'd previously been see in the area was suspected. Sienna had eagerly seized th chance to help when asked because finding it meant sh would no longer be an outcast. The Fae had cast her ou when she turned twenty-one because she was the bastar child of a sweet-faced Fae and a Draicon killer. But if sh found the Orb, Sienna could return to the only home she' own. It also meant she could recover her lost memories.

Every time she tried searching for her past, she met with closed door. Who was she? Which side ruled her?

Fae or Draicon?

Draicon, no way in hell.

Sensing someone staring, she glanced up, saw a man cross the aisle. He was heavily muscled and radiated power d confidence. Yet he also had the face of a gentle warrior. enna's breath caught. She felt a stir of sexual chemistry.

He was as lonely and grief stricken as she was. Her heart isted. Who had hurt this man? She wanted to go to him, mfort him and ease his sorrow. Sienna smiled.

An odd connection flared between them. Sienna locked her ze to his, desperately needing someone who understood.

Then her nostrils flared as she caught his scent. Hatred iled to the surface. Not a man. Draicon.

The enemy.

Find out what happens next in THE COVERT WOLF
by Bonnie Vanak.

Available August 2012 from Harlequin® Nocturne
wherever books are sold.

Harlequin Super Romance

*Enjoy a month of compelling, emotional stories, including
a poignant new tale of love lost and found from*

Sarah Mayberry

When Angela Bartlett loses her best friend to a rare heart
condition, it seems only natural that she step in and help
widower and friend Michael Young. The last thing she
expects is to find herself falling for him....

Within Reach

Available August 7!

"I loved it. I thought the story was very believable.
The characters were endearing. The author wrote beautifully...
I will be looking for future books by Sarah Mayberry."

–Sherry, Harlequin® Superromance® reader, on *Her Best Friend*

Find more great stories this month from
Harlequin® Superromance® at

www.Harlequin.com